Brody *couldn't* be prete
groom. That didn't ma

"You look like a million buck
dragons. "I'm sorry I wasn't
you woke up this morning."

Bea took a step back. Instead of his usual athletic wear, he had on a crisp, pale blue button-up shirt and jeans. The guy had more than his fair share of genetic gifts, and the work ethic to ensure he was still an elite athlete. Normally she didn't even notice, but with the way he was looking at her—with actual heat in his eyes—she saw him as the rest of the world probably did.

And wow, her bestie could be a hottie when he put his mind to it.

"I don't under—"

Brushing his thumb across her lips, he winked.

Her breath caught. Her thoughts followed, stuttering, getting hung up on that wink, on his touch.

And then he dropped a quick kiss to her mouth.

She almost fell over.

Rashida held up a hand. "Hang on. You aren't Jason."

"And thank God for that." He stuck out his hand. "Brody Emerson."

"But you're—" Rashida squinted at him and then looked at her clipboard "—you're the best man. *Man of honor*, rather."

Brody grinned widely, sucking the whole room into his charm. "Not anymore."

Dear Reader,

Lights, Camera...Wedding? is a best friends–to-lovers romance as well as a fake-engagement story, both at the top of my list of favorite tropes. I hope you love them, too. Best friends to lovers is particularly close to my heart, because it was the foundation of my own romance. My husband was one of my closest friends before we started dating in fourth-year university. I can vouch for the reality of all the should-we-shouldn't-we, will-we-wreck-what-we-have, what-do-I-do-with-these-feelings tension that makes these stories so delicious.

Pairing that with the wonderful are-we-going-to-get-caught mystery of a fake-engagement plot and the fun of wedding planning made for all sorts of laugh-out-loud escapades for Brody and Beatrix. They think they know everything about each other. Of course, they have a whole lot to learn about falling in love, especially while pretending to *be* in love—and while being filmed for a reality TV series, too! When their wedding of convenience reveals real feelings, can they risk their friendship and face past grief to find a lifetime of love?

Brody and Bea's story finishes the Hallorans' wedding lodge trilogy, but there are more Sutter Creek romances on the horizon (and a story in a brand-new location, too!). Be sure to visit my website, www.laurelgreer.com, where you'll find the latest news and a link to sign up for my newsletter. I'd love to hear your own real-life romance tropes—come say hello on Instagram or Facebook: @laurelgreerauthor.

Happy reading!

Laurel

Lights, Camera... Wedding?

LAUREL GREER

If you purchased this book without a cover you should be aware
that this book is stolen property. It was reported as "unsold and
destroyed" to the publisher, and neither the author nor the
publisher has received any payment for this "stripped book."

HARLEQUIN®
SPECIAL
EDITION™

PLEASE RECYCLE · THIS PRODUCT IS RECYCLABLE

Recycling programs
for this product may
not exist in your area.

ISBN-13: 978-1-335-72434-2

Lights, Camera...Wedding?

Copyright © 2022 by Lindsay Macgowan

All rights reserved. No part of this book may be used or reproduced in
any manner whatsoever without written permission except in the case of
brief quotations embodied in critical articles and reviews.

This is a work of fiction. Names, characters, places and incidents
are either the product of the author's imagination or are used fictitiously.
Any resemblance to actual persons, living or dead, businesses,
companies, events or locales is entirely coincidental.

For questions and comments about the quality of this book,
please contact us at CustomerService@Harlequin.com.

Harlequin Enterprises ULC
22 Adelaide St. West, 41st Floor
Toronto, Ontario M5H 4E3, Canada
www.Harlequin.com

Printed in U.S.A.

USA TODAY bestselling author **Laurel Greer** loves writing about all the ways love can change people for the better, especially when messy families and charming small towns are involved. She lives outside of Vancouver, BC, with her law-talking husband and two daughters, and is never far from a cup of tea, a good book or the ocean—preferably all three. Find her at www.laurelgreer.com.

Books by Laurel Greer

Harlequin Special Edition

Sutter Creek, Montana

What to Expect When She's Expecting
From Exes to Expecting
A Father for Her Child
Holiday by Candlelight
Their Nine-Month Surprise
In Service of Love
Snowbound with the Sheriff
Twelve Dates of Christmas
Lights, Camera...Wedding?

Visit the Author Profile page at Harlequin.com.

For Rob, still the best friend and partner
after twenty years, and the one who knows the
answer to that bit of ours I poached for chapter nine.

Prologue

"I've made a terrible mistake," Bea Halloran moaned. Holding one sparkly high heel in each hand, she shook them in the direction of her tablet screen. The device leaned against one of the three massive suitcases she was filling with half her wardrobe.

Brody Emerson's dry expression filled the screen, his mouth its usual *not-another-shoemergency* grimace. "Maybe not a world-peace-level crisis, Bea?"

She made a face at her best friend—the person she trusted more than anyone in the world.

Except her fiancé. Maybe.

She'd been joined at the hip with Brody ten times as long as she'd been with Jason, so there was a level of comfort there, an innate, gut-level knowing, that she still didn't have with the man she planned to wed.

Something to develop over a lifetime. It was okay to learn about one's partner over the course of a marriage, right?

Brody, on the other hand—no mysteries there. And she'd listened to enough rowing minutiae over the last twenty years to fill a four-inch binder, so she didn't feel too bad harassing him about her footwear dilemma.

"Two glittery pairs seemed the right call when I was out shopping, but now I'm thinking I should have gone for simple and flat. Black and brown," she said. "*Maybe* red for the holiday theme. I'm going on a do-it-yourself wedding show, not *Real Housewives of Montana.*"

Brody ran a hand through his thick sandy-blond hair and shook his head. "I thought the production company gave you a packing list."

Somehow, when he reminded her of that, it didn't chafe her the way Jason's similar reminder had when he texted her twenty minutes ago.

"Sort of," she said. "They didn't go as far as stiletto color."

She deposited the shoes in one of the overflowing cases and picked up her packing list. The paper shook in her hand, blurring the neatly typed suggestions for what she'd need during the next two weeks. The minute Jason had complained about her teeny executive functioning weakness to one of *DIY I Do:*

Times Two's ever-helpful production assistants, the PA typed up a guide to everything Bea could possibly require during filming that production wouldn't supply. Holiday-themed wedding planning clothes. Outdoor apparel suitable for Montana in the winter. Fancier attire for the rehearsal, preferably in Christmas red and gold to match the wedding's theme.

The wedding dress Bea had to make herself to meet the criteria of the show, but that wasn't *quite* finished.

She winced at the screen.

Brody's show of faux agony faded into seriousness. "You've got this, Sparks."

A silly nickname, but better than her family's usual "endearment" for her, Bumble. Way better to be a flash of light, a fire starter, than a bumbling mess.

Except for those times where I've proven the latter.

Getting Posy, her florist shop, off the ground had made her keenly aware of details in a way she'd never forced herself to care about before. So far, she'd rocked the wedding plans. Yeah, there were still a hundred things to complete. But that would just give the crew more things to film once she was in Sutter Creek at her sister's wilderness wedding lodge, DIYing it on camera.

She couldn't bumble that. Not her wedding, or anything that would follow.

And as always, Brody's encouragement revved up her self-confidence.

"Yes, coach," she teased. He was a former Olympic rower—former *gold medalist*—and the current coach of the men's team at a Seattle university. He probably muttered pithy motivational wisdom in his sleep. He'd definitely sprinkle it on his Corn Flakes if he lowered himself to eating simple carbohydrates for breakfast.

He'd never teased Bea about being more of a dreamer than a planner, but her gummy bear habit was fair game.

"What about you?" she said. "Are you done packing? I made your boutonniere today." She'd never considered anyone else as her attendant—she couldn't get married without Brody being the first person at her side. He'd happily claimed the role of man of honor.

"You make boutonnieres this far out?"

"It won't wilt. It's nonperishable."

"Ah, yeah. Because of Mr. Marrying-a-Florist-but-Doesn't-Like-Flowers."

"Brody..." she warned. Someone staunchly opposed to getting married really didn't get a say in the marital plans of others. Brody had never hidden his thoughts on falling in love and getting married, which kept the questions about why the two of them had never tried dating to once or twice a week instead of constant. "We've been over this. I'm more than floral arrangements. And he and I don't need to have the same interests to get married."

Jason had announced early on in their relationship that he wasn't a flower guy. She tried not to be too hurt, since it was her literal livelihood, albeit one she'd only fallen in love with a couple of years ago and recently decided to turn into her career. It had taken her a while to find her place, which meant no end of grief throughout her twenties. But turning thirty, moving to Seattle, meeting Jason, starting her business… Her life was *finally* starting to fit into the Halloran family mold of working one's ass off at a purposeful job and pairing up with someone for the ride. Having a family eventually, too. Her sister was head over heels for the game warden in their close-knit Montana hometown, and her brother and his wife were raising the cutest twins to walk the earth. In marrying Jason, Bea would finally fit in.

Bea knew the look on Brody's face well. Equal parts "Anyone wanting to get married is asking for it" and "Are you sure you want to make a lifetime commitment to *that* guy?"

She wished he was in the room with her so she could crumple her packing list and flick it at his head.

He rubbed his face with both hands and mumbled something she couldn't catch. Nor was she going to ask for clarification—she could guess at the sentiment.

"No raining your anti-marriage propaganda over my big week," she ordered. "You promised. I'm going to need you in my corner—over text, anyway—until you make your way home on Wednesday." Brody would participate in the filming, but only on the night before for the rehearsal and the actual day.

"I am always in your corner."

"I know. I'd be a mess without you." *No.* She needed to stop thinking like that. She could clean up her messes herself.

"I take it Jason's working late?" Brody said. "He's not helping you pack?"

"I didn't need him to." She managed to still her hand enough to glance from the beginning to the end of the list. "I think I have everything."

Most certainly inaccurate. She always forgot something when she traveled.

Time to break that streak.

"If you forget something, I can bring it with me," he offered.

"Thanks, but I need to appear competent from moment one. When Jason and I step off the plane tomorrow, the cameras will be on. I'll need to be put together in a way I've never managed before."

DIY I Do: Times Two was a massively popular StreamFlix show, based around the idea that a similar wedding theme could be executed with a large budget or a small one. She and Jason had successfully bid to be the extravagant example, for the special Christmas episode, no less. When it aired, it would boost Bea's florist shop into the Seattle stratosphere. The business her sister Emma owned with her fiancé would benefit, too. Emma and Luke— Brody's cousin, incidentally—owned the newly renovated Moosehorn River Lodge, and Emma had plans to turn it into a luxe wedding destination. The producers couldn't stop gushing about the glam-in-the-woods setting being perfect for an upscale wedding with rustic touches. With StreamFlix as the platform, Bea and Emma couldn't lose on the publicity front.

Having the production budget cover the ever-inflating wedding bill was a bonus, too, given Bea was strapped for cash after pouring everything she had—and lots she didn't—into Posy.

"Pardon me for disagreeing," Brody said, "but I like how you're put together. Emma and Nora already have the market cornered on Halloran sisters who dream about spreadsheets and day planners. I love how you bring some spontaneity into the world."

You're pretty much the only one.

"What plans are you changing now?" Jason's stiff voice came from behind her.

She jumped, dropping the paper. She whirled to face him. "Nothing's changing. I'm doing a final check to make sure I have everything."

"Given you've packed half the contents of our condo, I don't see what you could be missing," Jason said woodenly.

His undone tie was the only sign he'd been at the office for twelve hours. Otherwise, he was completely put together. His short blond hair swooped precisely to the side; the only creases in his suit were the ones put there by the dry cleaner. Some days, it was surprising he didn't literally shine, he was so polished. Her opposite, really, which was a good thing. They balanced each other out. She helped him think big and relax, and he helped her focus on a single path.

He seemed unfazed that he'd startled the living bejesus out of her. She was willing to cut him some slack—the mess in the bedroom *was* tease-worthy, and he'd been completely supportive of her getting-married-on-TV gambit.

She flung her arms around him. "One day closer to getting married!"

He was as stiff as a bundle of wire flower stems.

"What's wrong?" Had he heard Brody's dig about him working late?

"We need to talk," he said, an edge to the voice she'd first fallen in love with two years ago when he'd ordered a milkshake from her struggling ice cream truck and then offered to take her out for dinner that night. Usually, his words came out confident. Tonight, they were plain brisk.

Alarm rang through her. She exchanged a quick glance with on-screen Brody.

Concern filled her best friend's brown eyes. "How about I leave you two to it? Call me when you get to Montana." He gave her a little salute and then the Call Ended by Host notification popped up.

She sat on the edge of the bed and played with the hem of her tulle skirt. She hadn't worn tutu-style anything since she quit her short-lived job as a theme park princess years ago, but she'd found the flouncy garment when she was digging in the back of her closet and decided it might look fun on camera.

Jason's serious expression, however, was the opposite of fun.

"Did the stock market crash or something? You look miserable," she said.

His mouth flattened. "I *am* miserable."

Her heart caught in her throat. "Why?"

"This!" He waved a hand at the suitcases and the boxes of florist supplies and wedding paraphernalia, ending his gesture with a flourish in her direction.

Uh, excuse me? "What, you don't like the wedding plans? Or my skirt?"

"It's not your *skirt*, Beatrix. It's…it's *you*."

Her face went numb. She couldn't have heard that right. Her lips felt like rubber cement, flapping uselessly. "Me?"

He jammed his fingers into his hair. "Crap, not exactly. It's you *and* it's me. Or rather, that we're so different. I thought we could work with that. But the closer we get to our wedding, the sillier you've gotten with preparing for this damn show, I realize we can't."

She couldn't decide which of his words she needed to focus on most. "You think I'm *silly*?"

He sat on the end of the bed. Not close to her, like he might if he were trying to make things better. Two feet away, gripping the comforter and staring at the floor with the singular focus of a man who'd apparently just figured out he proposed to a person he considered a joke.

The mattress didn't make a sound as he sat. Pretty sure it had cost more than her aging Volkswagen Beetle. Moving into Jason's condo had come with a big jump in thread count and a killer view. It never felt entirely like home, which she always thought was her issue, her self-esteem.

Maybe it *wasn't* actually home. Had she sensed something neither of them had figured out until now?

"I can't marry you," he said.

The staccato syllables dug into her like shrapnel.

"We have to get married," she said. "We have a contract with *DIY I Do*. And my shop and the lodge are depending on this—"

"And none of that has to do with us being in love!" Face flushed, he tugged at the collar of his shirt hard enough to pop a button.

Her heart was beating a thousand miles a minute. "Of course we're in love."

His gaze collided with hers. "Are we?"

We have to be.

This was her chance to squash her mercurial nature that stopped everyone from taking her seriously. What was more serious than marrying an investment banker?

"Bea." He reached for her hand. "Be honest with yourself."

She snatched her fingers away. "Telling *myself* things is the least of my worries. What am I going to tell my family, our friends, the production crew? And breaking the contract won't be cheap."

Those shouldn't be her biggest concerns. They shouldn't overshadow the loss of the man who was supposed to be the love of her life.

Were they?

Sludgy guilt slicked her insides. It couldn't be true.

"Why now?" she pressed.

"I thought I could do it. But this week, dozens of my coworkers have asked me if I'm excited to get married. And every time, when I said 'yeah,' I wanted to puke. When my boss told me to leave the office to finish packing this evening, I had to run for my garbage can the minute he stepped out the door." Air shuddered from his lips. "Is my timing bad? Sure. It's necessary, though. Better now than after we complete more filming, or after we exchange vows. Make up whatever story that suits you. Blame me." He stood. "I'll cover my half of the costs."

"Do you understand how much we'll owe if we don't go through with a wedding? The food, the flowers, decor for the entire lodge. Chantilly lace and truffles. Travel bills." Her head was starting to spin. "And it's not just the ceremony. It's a whole weekend of events. Not to mention the cost of ten days of shutting down most of the lodge for Luke and Emma—"

He scoffed. "Your sister's not going to charge us."

"How could she not? It's a week and a half of income! She can't snap her fingers and fill rooms."

"Christ, whatever. I'll pay half of that, too."

"Leaving me with the rest!" She swallowed, trying

to temper her tone from shriek to calm. "You're well aware I can't afford that."

"We took a risk on this, Bea. You read the contract just like I did." So calm. Bored, almost. If she didn't know better, she'd think he was delivering a monthly report, not jilting his bride the week before the wedding.

"It's not the contract that's letting me down, it's *you*."

Pinching the bridge of his nose, he stood. "I'll go to a hotel for a night or two so you have time to pack your things."

Wait. Packing? She held up a hand. "You're kicking me out?"

"It's...not your place."

Ouch. But...of course. The condo was in his name, not hers.

"Right. Should have been another sign, I guess? That the sum total of my possessions I bothered to unpack is my French press and a handful of books on the shelf?" Humiliation engulfed her. "I'm supposed to go to Montana tomorrow. *We* are supposed to go."

He shook his head slowly. "Go if you need to. Use the storage unit for as long as you need it. I won't do anything to your stuff."

Mainly because it's not as nice as your own stuff.

Had he always only tolerated her presence?

"I'm not using your fricking storage unit." She jolted to her feet. "Give me two hours. I already packed a lot of my clothes and personal items. I'll bag the rest up and keep it in my office at the shop. And I'll take the hotel room tonight. I don't want to spend another minute in *your* condo."

"Okay." That weird, cold tone again. She hated it.

She wished Brody hadn't hung up. That he'd witnessed this, heard the blow-by-blow, so that she didn't have to recap it for him. The thought of explaining this to the people she loved made her want to puke, and Brody would be able to tell if she edited the sordid tale.

Unless he was furious with her for jeopardizing his cousin's business...

She started shaking. Holy God. What were Emma and Luke going to do? Talk about people taking a risk—they had, on *her.*

She'd have to face them and tell them the truth tomorrow. And the production team. The host had been so kind. Would they have some sort of backup plan?

Her disbelief hardened to anger. "I'd complain that you're leaving me to deal with the fallout, but at least it will save me from having to see your face." She spat it more than said it.

How had she gone from wanting to spend the rest of her life with this man to not wanting to be in his presence?

Her knees were jelly, but she needed to buck up, find a solution.

"It was your idea. It's not my mess to clean up," Jason said. "Unless you avoid it and flit off to something different like you usually do."

"You...you said you liked that I was a free spirit," she said, words strangled. "Said I brought surprise to your life."

"And I decided it's not a trait I want to live with." He looked away. It was close to an eye roll.

How dare he! She'd built up a good wall against people who didn't appreciate her for who she was, but that hammer left a crack.

Maybe the fact it didn't demolish you is a sign?

Maybe. She straightened her shoulders. "Don't get me wrong—I think this is cruel timing. You signed on just as much as I did. It's *not* my problem alone. But other than that? You're doing me a big favor. I don't want to marry someone who looks down on me."

If I wanted to live with constant criticism, I never would have left home.

Come to think of it, he'd been flinging passive-aggressive frustration at her for a couple of months now, and she was so conditioned to accept it that she'd barely processed his increasing unhappiness. She could admit that to herself *and* acknowledge he was a massive jerk.

She flicked her hand in the universal gesture for "you're dismissed."

"Bea—"

"Nope. I have to keep packing."

Except, instead of for two weeks and a wedding, she was packing up her whole life.

Again.

Chapter One

Brody found nothing so jarring as having near-constant communication lines severed with no notice. He sipped his coffee in the airy kitchen of his Seattle town house and glared at his cell screen. He'd woken up early, worrying about Bea. Texted a bunch. Even called.

No replies.

Concern tightened his chest. He'd suspected things were hinky last night when he'd witnessed—over Zoom, anyway—Jason arrive home. He'd heard nothing the rest of the night from her, and nothing this morning, either. No answer. What the hell had gone on? She and Jason were supposed to get on a plane at two o'clock.

He shot her off another *where are you?* before heading out for a run, even though he'd trained hard the previous evening with some of his athletes. He wasn't sure he was physically capable of running fast enough to escape his thoughts, but trying was preferable to sitting at home fretting.

Also preferable to hunting Jason down and giving the guy a piece of his mind for that dismissive crack about Bea having packed up half their condo. Probably with his hand around the other man's throat, so yeah, best he stayed far away from Bea's fiancé.

He was looping around Green Lake when a text arrived from his cousin Luke.

Have you heard from Bea?

Brody winced, slowing his strides. Luke, their grandfather and Bea's sister Emma co-owned the lodge where Bea was supposed to get married, though the transition to a wedding facility was mostly Emma's baby. She was no doubt spinning off the planet with everything the upcoming nuptials would demand, and being engaged to Luke, he'd be her main sounding board.

Brody typed with one eye on the path ahead so as not to trip. Not since last night. Is something wrong?

Luke: She's gone radio silent. Emma's freaking out.

Good to know he wasn't the only one overreacting, then.

Unless they weren't overreacting.

Brody: She had a wedding order to complete this morning. She's probably finishing it. Or packing.

Bea dreamed big and struggled to plan, which often overwhelmed her. Maybe she needed a hand… And God knew Jason wouldn't think to offer one. He was probably at his office, leaving her to deal with all the last-minute organization.

She was the kind of woman that, if a person was foolish enough to want to fall in love, they'd better hang on for dear life because she was a goddamn rainbow among storm clouds. The sheer joy she surrounded herself with as she barreled her way through whatever caught her interest at any given time was enough to power a city block. Hell, even the dregs of that joy would do it. Jason seemed to make her happy enough, but Brody suspected he didn't appreciate her like she deserved.

An opinion he hadn't kept secret from her. But he'd also wanted to maintain their close friendship, so when it had become clear they disagreed on whether Jason was a good partner, Brody had said his piece and then agreed to her request to leave it alone.

Should he have? Should he push harder, save Bea from eventual heartache? Not just because Jason wasn't her equal, but because marriage, commitment even, made a person too vulnerable.

He'd picked his mom up off the floor too many times to believe getting married was worth the heartache.

He blocked out the rush of the past before it could take over his thoughts.

Compartmentalizing, like he'd had to do to win races and medals and his coveted coaching position.

Or avoidance, given I'm not racing anymore.

Gritting his teeth and ignoring the voice that liked to pop in his head at the worst times, he slowed to a walk and typed another message to his cousin. I'm worried about her.

Luke: Yeah? You've always told me she can handle anything.

True. Ever since ten-year-old Bea showed up on Brody's doorstep after his dad died, he'd been going along with her adventures. Following his little sparkler of a neighbor had changed his life more than any other decision he'd made. One hazy summer day she'd barreled onto his front porch, announcing she'd found an ancient map and needed his help to hunt down what was certainly lost treasure, and that he could be sad while he was doing it, but he had to come outside. Trailing after her into the woods surrounding the lodge had only scratched the surface of the places she'd eventually dragged him to.

Over time, he'd had his own things going on, too—competing internationally in a sport was no small thing. But regardless of whether she was in Costa Rica or Orlando—or just down the block in Seattle, trying and failing to get a gourmet ice cream truck off the ground—she'd cast rays of light into the shadows of his life. The ones that had rolled in like a hurricane when two uniformed people showed up on that same front porch.

She'd shown him how to be happy again. He hated seeing her anything less than the same, and her silence suggested things hadn't gone well last night.

Another text landed on-screen a second later, finally from Bea.

Can I get a ride to the airport?

I? Just her?
Of course. What time? What's going on? he replied.

Three little dots floated. He ran the equivalent of a few blocks while he waited for her to finish typing.

Her message finally appeared. In two hours, please.

Muscles jittering from the frustration of her half-assed response, he picked up to a jog again. The damp November air left a sheen of mist on his face.

Brody: Sparks, I'm worried. What's happening?

After another minute, he called. No answer.

Well, now he was getting annoyed. Why did she need a ride? Was she going alone? Had Jason decided to stay in Seattle longer and not to take part in the wedding preamble?

Or is he canceling the wedding entirely?

Goddamn...

He didn't want to think that was the case. For all his hesitation about Bea's fiancé, he didn't *want* her to get her heart broken.

Okay, time for a plan, to be prepared for any outcome. He hadn't intended to head to Sutter Creek until Wednesday night, but his gut had nudged him long ago to book off the whole week from work, just in case. He was grateful that last week had been the final fall regatta—he hadn't felt guilty about arranging with his assistant coach to take over training their team. Better yet, he didn't need to feel guilty about changing his flight from Wednesday to now.

Whatever was going on with Bea and Jason, she might need support, and hell, he never minded a few extra days with his family.

He cut down the next path to the road—the quickest route home. He had an airport ride to provide and a suitcase to pack.

Bea carefully wrapped silk ribbon around the thick bunch of stems, folded the end and secured it with pearl-tipped straight pins. Tears pricked her eyes. If she went the rest of her life without holding a bridal bouquet again, that would be great.

Could a person run a successful florist business without doing flowers for weddings? Her upcoming schedule said no, but a woman could hope.

Or maybe she should leave it all behind. Walk away from the shop, move back to Montana and work for her sister or her parents until something new came around that lit her soul on fire…

Her stomach lurched.

No. She'd walked away from too many things, too many times. And usually, crafting floral masterpieces filled her well.

Just not the day after getting dumped.

By a man who didn't light my soul on fire.

The crap timing of the breakup might be on Jason, but she was just as much at fault for the rest of it. She'd ignored blatant signs that she was making a mistake, and now she had a giant stack of garbage bags and boxes to show for it.

Packing had taken a lot longer than the two hours she'd predicted. She'd kept thinking she'd taped up the last container or fastened the last twist tie and then remembered something else she'd squirreled away, usually at the back of a cupboard behind something sleeker and fancier of Jason's. Her small office, to the left of her biggest storage cooler, was now overflowing with all the possessions she wasn't bringing to Montana.

Dazed and sleep-deprived, she blinked at the final

order she had to fulfill before slinking back to Montana with her tail between her legs. The standard checklist she made sure to check three times every morning of a delivery sat next to the shallow box holding the bridesmaids' bouquets.

Given the bride wasn't pretending her mid-November wedding was actually happening at Christmas, like Bea and Jason would have done, the colors were lime and pink with some cream to ground it all.

Sending thanks to the Starbucks mermaid for the existence of triple-shot venti macchiatos, Bea took a long swig of her coffee and cross-referenced her list to her notes. Organization wasn't second, third or even fourth nature, but she needed to do it to succeed at something she loved doing in a way she'd never managed to do before.

Thankfully, there were a lot of pretty highlighters and pens to liven up the tedium.

She picked a thick-tipped fountain pen filled with fuchsia ink and got to it.

Bride's bouquet—check.

Extra dahlias in the maid of honor's bouquet—check.

Six identical large posies for the bridesmaids.

Two smaller ones for her client's nieces, and a box of glitter-doused petals for the nephew, who reportedly wanted nothing more than to fling "unicorn kisses" all the way down the aisle.

A lump formed in Bea's throat.

Jason's niece would have been their flower girl. Not with anything so déclassé as glitter. That was a direct quote from Jason's mom, who'd made it more than clear she was appalled her son's wedding would be televised. But Bea had planned to make every petal and delicate leaf beautiful.

If only she'd spent more time thinking about actually getting married to Jason rather than the bouquet she'd planned to carry down the aisle. She'd hurt them both in her carelessness.

And she'd hooped herself financially by signing the contract with the streaming service. Her stomach twisted at the deposit she now owed on those flowers. As the high-expense event for the Christmas episode of *DIY I Do: Times Two*, she'd planned for the swankiest flower suite of her career to date. The host-producers had loved that she'd be doing the flowers herself.

Jason's mom, who'd totally missed the do-it-yourself angle of the show, had sniffed and asked, "Are you sure you don't want to hire someone more experienced, Beatrice?"

Her fiancé *had* corrected his mother on Bea's name, but he hadn't taken the time to defend her craft.

Ugh, he was no doubt headed to his family's country club for lunch now, where they'd all sit around, tittering about how he'd dodged a bullet, and what had he been thinking, getting engaged to someone who dared show up for dinner in something other than navy, tan or twinsets?

Nor did she have the time to concern herself with the inevitable celebrations the Doucette-Smythes would throw over their son being free from her clutches. She had her own family to deal with.

Should she have called them right away after Jason had walked out? Maybe. But she'd been numb, and packing, and it seemed like news best delivered in person.

Or you're putting it off.

That, too.

Focus, Beatrix. The list.

Right. Ten boutonnieres. Two, four, six, eight— nine. One short? *Damn it.*

Hands shaking, she ran to her cooler. *Oh please, oh please, let there be one more succulent.* The part-time employee she'd hired on in the summer was going to be keeping the shop open for the two weeks Bea would be in Montana, which meant the cooler was still full of flowers. The greenery was on one of the shelves at the back. Hopefully Sanjana hadn't used up all the Kermit mums for the tabletop decorations she'd delivered to the wedding facility yesterday.

Bea peered around a bucket of gerbera daisies and a completed arrangement for a funeral home, and…

Yes. Victory. A dozen stems of the light green, tight-petaled blooms hid behind some purple-tipped amaranth, along with the lime leaves she'd ordered special for today's client's wedding.

Hands full of greenery, she went out to the front counter and started assembling. Her hands shook, throwing off her usually steady detail work. Every time she'd ended up leaving one of her other attempts at finding her life's passion, she'd come back to this, working for florists or in greenhouses and garden centers. It had been Brody who'd pointed out that flowers could *be* her passion, if she wanted them to be.

Were they? Maybe. She enjoyed the variety of it, certainly. It wasn't hours upon hours of hugging sticky, overstimulated children while their parents jostled for pictures in front of a magical castle. Definitely wasn't like Costa Rica, standing behind a desk listening to complaints from tourists who were supposed to be blissed-out from being at a nature retreat. Or the literal manure shoveling her eldest sister did at the family ranch—no, thank you. And while she'd enjoyed scooping ice cream for smiling faces around the city, she'd quickly drowned in red ink. What she really wanted was to be able to say she'd held down a job or successfully run a business for five, even ten years without feeling the urge to leave or the necessity to sell.

Flowers. Flowers will do it. She'd balanced her books—barely—and was even managing to keep on an employee.

The doorbell chimed.

She kept her eyes on the stems she was wrapping with florist tape. "Almost done here, Florence, just a quick wrap of twine to cover the tape and—"

"You didn't answer my last text." Not Florence, the bridesmaid in charge of picking up the flowers for today's bride. "Or my calls."

Concern rent Brody's low, soft accusation.

She jerked her gaze to his, keeping her mouth flat. "I had ten bouquets to finish off."

He strode across the rough wood floor, gaze narrowed and posture stiff. "You asked me for a ride to the airport and then ghosted me."

"You said you could take me." She resumed her twisting. "That was all I needed to know."

His wide rower's hands flattened on the other side of the counter. "And I needed to know why."

She studied the final boutonniere. "This is imbalanced somehow. I can't sell something that isn't right—"

"Don't change the subject. What happened?"

"What happened? I forgot a boutonniere." A hot tear dripped down her cheek, but her hands were full, and she couldn't wipe it away. "And now I had to rush this one, and the proportions are off—"

"Beatrix." He tipped her chin up with a finger and wiped her tear away with a thumb. "Boutonnieres don't make you cry."

"No, but getting dumped does."

She'd never seen him move so fast. Not during a race or jumping off a podium or running wind sprints with his crew. He was around the counter and had her in a safe, steel-band hug before she could blink.

Oh wow, not having to hold herself up was nice. She let herself sag in his arms. His muscles barely flinched.

"Go ahead," she said, words muffled against his thin puffer-style jacket. "I deserve an 'I told you so.'"

"No. I wanted to be wrong." Unlike Jason's quiet, unsettling tone last night, Brody's murmur, even filled with regret, brought the first ounce of calm she'd felt since her world tipped upside down.

She'd been trying to hold back her tears, stay strong, but what was the point? It would be better to let loose now rather than in front of her family and the production crew.

One tear fell, then a second, then a flood, until a salad plate–sized wet spot stained the front of his teal-colored jacket. Recovering, she grabbed a tissue and dabbed at the dampness.

"Don't you have any clothes without the university logo on them?"

He stroked her hair, bringing her head back to his chest. "Yes, the ones with the USRowing logo."

She laughed. Her throat was a little raw from crying so hard. "Thank you for—"

The doorbell tinkled, interrupting her.

A short East Asian woman bounced in, her long hair up in an intricate knot of curls and loops. Bea had met her before, when the bride had come in to confirm an order, and the three of them had ended up chatting about Bea's own wedding.

"You look gorgeous, Florence," Bea said, wiping her eyes.

The bridesmaid stared intently at Bea's face. "What's wrong? It's not Jessica's flowers, is it?"

"No, I think the order's perfect."

"Sorry you're having some other hiccup, then." Pink lips, color chosen to complement the dahlias in the bouquets, twitched on one side. "At least you have a fiancé who's willing to dry your tears."

Bea stepped back, for a second seeing Brody as the world did, not as a platonic friend of two decades. Tall and broad with an angular face that had looked right at home on magazine covers and television features after winning gold. And those brown eyes that always held the promise of a good time. She knew that good time never went beyond hugs and comfort but could see why Florence had misunderstood.

"Oh, Brody's not my fiancé. I don't—" No point in putting a damper on the morning with explanations of broken engagements or details on how she'd promised herself long ago that she'd never let herself fall in love with Brody. At least she'd successfully saved herself that particular pain. "That's neither here nor there. I so hope Jessica's wedding day goes off without a hitch."

That Jessica's groom didn't decide she was silly and not worth his time.

Sniffling, she finished up the transaction and

waved Florence on her way. Brody helped carry the flowers outside. When he returned, he looked as serious as he had when they'd first become friends— a twelve-year-old kid grieving the loss of his dad.

"What the hell happened with Jason?" he asked.

Right. She'd been crying so hard, she hadn't explained herself.

The story spilled out, hot and scalding like her earlier weepfest.

Brody crossed his arms. His muscles bulged and his pressed-together lips paled.

His knowing brown gaze was too much to take. She buried her face in her hands.

"I told myself I was in love with him. I'm not sure that was true," she said. "I'll fix it. I have to. I owe the production company a chunk of change. Luke and Emma, too, for their lost bookings. And growing Posy without *DIY I Do*? If I'll even be able to afford to keep it afloat given all the money I'll owe."

"Bea…"

"How am I going to face them all?" she whispered. "I'm going to walk into my parents' house and they're all going to wonder what I did to screw up this time…"

"No way. They give you too hard a time some days, and that's unfair. But they do love you. They'll support you."

"How do you know?"

"Because you didn't do anything wrong." A big palm splayed across her head, stroking her hair. "It'll be okay."

She brushed his hand away. Who knew what her chin-length curls looked like after hours of packing and bouquet touch-ups? Before she boarded the plane, she'd have to unearth one of the rainbow of slouchy beanies Brody had knit for her over the years. Cover up the evidence of her lack of sleep.

"The showrunners don't love me, though," she said. "Who knows how they'll react?"

He squeezed her shoulders, grounding her like he always managed to do. "Want me to come?"

She knew he would. And the thought of having someone at her side who was fully in her corner was super tempting. Except…

"It's not your job to hop on a plane this time." Helping her move from Costa Rica to Orlando, and then less than a year later from Orlando to Seattle… Three rescues like that would be too many. "I need to prove I can follow through on this. Even though it's not going to be the success I hoped."

Gathering her things, she did what she needed to lock up and motioned Brody toward the door. She carted her suitcase out.

He eyed her single piece of luggage. "Where's all the rest of your stuff? I swear you had three suitcases and four boxes while you were packing last night."

"That's all in my office, along with everything else I own. I spent most of the night moving things from my—Jason's—place. And there's no point hauling any of it to Montana. I won't need all the wedding supplies or my dress."

"Wait, did you sleep here? You should have called. My guest room is yours whenever you need it."

She shook her head. She hadn't been ready to face anyone. "I dozed in my office chair for an hour, but then I needed to get straight to work. It was fine."

He sent her a look that said *it's the opposite of fine* and pressed a button on his fob to open the hatch. The door lifted. A large duffel bag occupied one side of the trunk.

She cocked an eyebrow at him. Had he jammed his hands in his pockets and started whistling, he couldn't have looked guiltier.

"I already changed my flight," he said. "I'm on the same one as you."

The same flight? "But you didn't know what happened. Why would you think you needed to come?"

Bracing a hand on the door of the hatch, he said, "Gut feeling, I guess."

Her own gut wobbling from exhaustion and unsure how to process his unilateral decision, she made her way to the passenger seat.

A bulk bag of organic gummy bears from the health food store across the street sat on the console, next to a golden latte in the cupholder.

He pointed to it. "For you."

Her heart went a little mushy. "Thank you."

"I know changing my flight smacks of domineering, but I can't regret doing it. Especially now. You need a friend."

"No, Brody, I need a fiancé."

He reached over and squeezed her hand, his fingers strong and calloused from spending most of his life with an oar in his grip.

Comforting.

Not a solution. She hadn't been kidding—what she needed was a groom. She didn't *want* one. The thought of getting married turned her stomach at the moment. But the possibility of financial ruin was even worse.

"Ugh, why did I have to apply to have my wedding be the deluxe version?"

He winced. "What's the bill going to be?"

She gave him her estimate of half the costs. "It's in the contract that the production company only pays for the actual wedding expenses if the event goes through."

"Ouch. You never told me about that clause." A dark blond brow lifted. "Was that on purpose?"

Maybe. He would have recommended caution, for sure. Her cheeks heated. "Reality TV contracts are typically harsh. We had an entertainment lawyer look at it. It's not a standard inclusion, but it's not unheard of. I knew what I was taking on."

His expression darkened. "You weren't expecting Jason to bail on you. I'm not going to pretend I had a high opinion of him, but even I didn't think he'd do this."

Ugh. If she could disappear into the leather passenger seat, she would. "I really wish he'd gone through with the wedding so that he wasn't leaving me with my share of the bill. *DIY I Do* needs an ultrafancy, romantic wedding. I'm not sure they care what happens after the fact."

"Like you'd want to be around Jason right now." Another hand squeeze, and a gentle smile. "That would have been miserable, Sparks."

She flinched. The nickname didn't feel right today. She was devoid of creativity, of solutions. "I guess. I just— It's beyond frustrating to be so close and to end up with a towering pile of manure."

"I bet."

"If this was a blockbuster rom-com, I'd hire an escort to stand in as my groom." She could see it put to film, her inevitably cast as a manic pixie dream girl, showing up with a delicious Marvel superhero actor on her arm. He'd charm the production team, her family and her—eventually into bed, please and thank you, given she was a sucker for biceps and self-deprecating humor...

Wait.

She whipped her gaze toward Brody, who had a wrist on the steering wheel and a hand on the shifter.

He had biceps and self-deprecating humor. *He* could charm a production team, and her family already loved him.

And as long as it was clear she didn't expect him to tumble with her into bed, and his obligations would end the minute the cameras stopped rolling...

A flash of inspiration burned away some of her dread.

"Brody, will you marry me?"

Chapter Two

White flashed in Brody's side-view mirror, and a car horn let out a prolonged honk.

"Jesus!" He righted the wheel, just managing to avoid sideswiping a delivery van. His vehicle lurched. So did his stomach.

Bea shrieked and grabbed the ceiling handle with one hand and his shoulder with the other.

Ragged breaths sawed out of his chest. He gripped the steering wheel, trying to keep the car between the lane lines. "Oh man. I'm sorry."

"No, *I'm* sorry. I never should have asked you that, let alone while you're driving." The hand on his shoulder tightened for a second before she let go, crossed her arms and dropped her head against the headrest.

"Talk about an embodiment of *all* the impulsive decision-making I'm trying to avoid."

Right. Nearly totaling his SUV had made him momentarily forget that his best, always platonic friend had just proposed to him.

His heart beat an insistent rhythm.

Will.

You.

Marry.

Me?

Yeah, no. He'd never let himself be that vulnerable with another person, as vulnerable as his mom had been. "You know me. I'm not marriage material."

She groaned. "I didn't mean a *real* marriage. Just that, if I *was* going to show up with a fake groom, you'd be the most logical choice." An uncomfortable laugh bubbled from her lips. "But you're right. Fake or not, it's a ridiculous idea."

His pulse calmed by another few beats. "I don't mind you spitballing, Bea. Not with a bill that large hanging over your head."

He knew Posy needed the publicity boost, and Bea needed not to go into debt over a canceled wedding. So did Emma and Luke, for that matter. He didn't see either of them accepting any money from Bea for the two weeks of lost revenue, meaning they'd be out half that amount, provided they made Jason pony up for his part.

He cautiously changed lanes, heading toward the

freeway. "A fake groom isn't a preposterous idea, in and of itself. Reality TV is all about being fake."

"I don't think that's the case for *DIY I Do*. When I met the host-producers for filming all the preamble stuff that one day, they were really passionate about having a show that was real." Her breath hitched. "One of the reasons I wanted to be on the show. They made it seem so romantic."

God, he hated the misery on her face, and the inability to do a thing to erase it, to fix the root cause. He had some savings, but not near what she owed.

And like she'd said, for the show to go on, she needed a fiancé.

It wasn't like there was a way a person could pick a bridegroom in the right age, size and shape. If she was really considering having a fiancé who wasn't Jason, one who could convince the production crew, it would need to be someone who knew everything about her.

And if someone had earned a master's degree in all things Bea Halloran, it was him. He'd seen every part of her over the years.

Well, not *every* part.

She'd stripped down emotionally for him, but their intimacy had always ended there.

Objectively, yeah, she was stunning. From her sunshine curls to her dimples, her magnetic green eyes to the tilt of her smile, a man could lose days of his life taking in all of Bea Halloran.

He'd vowed long ago to ignore all that. They would

always, always be platonic. Siblings, without the family politics.

Except if they pretended to get married, it could salvage the whole shebang.

"You know," he said, keeping his words casual as he checked over his shoulder and changed lanes. "Back at the shop, your client mistook us for a couple."

Her glossy pink lips twisted in amusement. "That's nothing new."

"Right. Which means people who don't know us easily believe we're together. Tell the world we're engaged, and everyone would believe it."

She swatted his leg. "I told you, I wasn't serious."

Was he really going to do this? Accept his best friend's proposal?

He swallowed, expecting a thunderclap from the heavens, scolding him for being absurd—or at least a jolt of nerves, a zap from his own conscience—but nothing happened. "Seems like the *exact* time to be serious. With the financial concerns you mentioned, you're in a pour-on-the-gas-in-the-final-five-hundred-meters situation. The desperation zone. So yeah, if it keeps you out of debt and salvages your pride, I'll be your husband-to-be for a couple of weeks."

In the corner of his vision, he saw her jaw drop. He shot her a smile and turned down the next cross street, away from the freeway exit.

"Wait, where are we going?"

"Back to Posy to fetch your extra suitcases and boxes."

"Wait, no." She gripped his arm. "A fiancé doesn't do me much good. The show isn't *DIY Engagement*. It's *DIY I Do*. A key part of that is the *I do*. We can't pretend to get married, Brody."

"But—" There had to be a way.

"No, no 'but.' This show is about actual weddings. The license, the guests, the officiant—there's no way to fake all that."

Brody winced. "Good point. I didn't think it through past 'pretend.'"

"I don't think you thought it through *at all*. Because the contract costs are still going to exist when we don't go through with a wedding." Tears glittered in her eyes. "I need to put on my adulting pants this time. Spend some time being single, do some soul-searching about how I misread my feelings for Jason so badly. And then figure out a way to pay for my half of the wedding expenses without leaning on my family. No one is taking on my debt this time."

"You and Emma both took the risk on the show as a promotional opportunity, though."

"No, she took a risk on *me*. If anyone's business is going to flounder because of this, it's going to be mine." She frowned. "No one will be shocked if I go under yet again."

"You're not losing your shop."

"You say that as if there's a choice. If I have a huge sum to pay back, I won't be able to afford the rent."

"Bea…"

Lifting her chin, she wiped at a damp cheek with the back of her hand. "Turn the car around, Brody. What's one more unfinished project, one more career to toss on the funeral pyre?" She shook her head. "Why can't I make anything stick?"

He ignored her command. He'd get her to see this was actually possible.

"Maybe sticking to something as the sole measure of success is unfair," he said, voice rougher than he'd intended.

Because for all that Bea had her ephemeral moments, she brought joy into the world. Her kind of creative energy was vital.

"You—the man who reached the pinnacle of rowing and now helps others do the same—you are going to tell me sticking with something is overrated?"

He had done that. Not only had he dedicated his life to rowing, but he'd done it at the expense of almost everything else. Aside from his small number of friendships and his bonds with the few family members he had left, he'd shoved everything to the back burner during his training. It had given him a great excuse whenever his grandfather bugged him about not having a relationship that lasted longer than the life span of a housefly.

Through it all, Bea had been there for him. Flying to his regattas, propping him up during injuries, believing in him at his lowest moments.

He'd thought there wasn't a way to repay her for that, but maybe there was.

"You could make this stick, Bea. Let's do it for real." He cleared his throat, the words foreign on his tongue. "Get married."

She laughed.

Fair enough. On the surface, it *was* laughable. He'd been adamant he'd never get married, and when he made a decision, he stuck with it.

Except temporarily marrying Bea will work.

He'd always trusted his inner voice.

"I mean it, Sparks."

The disbelieving hilarity washed away as she straightened. "You don't want to get married, ever. Not for real."

"I don't. But if it's just temporary... For as long as it takes to fulfill your contract with *DIY I Do* and convince people after the fact that it was the real deal."

"And then my family would think I added you to the list of things I tried and tossed away," she said quietly.

He turned one last time, a few blocks down the street from Posy. "I'd make it clear it was me. No one's going to be surprised when I decide I *don't* want to stay married. You'd be debt-free and running your shop. *And* you'd still have me. Your best friend who you happened to exchange rings with one time."

She stared at him, blank for a moment. Then a hint of her usual sunshine, the smile that had the

power to improve any difficult day, flickered bright.
"You're serious."

"After, while we're waiting for the right time to
annul, you could live at my place. Live in my guest
room, split rent with me—saves you from finding
an apartment when you get home."

"Be…roommates?"

"Legally, we'd be married." He shot her a small
smile. "Isn't it common wisdom that you're supposed
to marry your best friend?"

"Not your *platonic* best friend. And not you."
She held up her fingers and hooked them into mock
quotes. "'Any woman who put a ring on my finger
would be a fool.'"

"If she was in love with me, yeah."

"And I'm not," she said softly.

"Of course you aren't." Thank Christ for that. He
parallel parked in front of Posy, shut off the engine
and took her hands. Soft but strong—the kind of
hands a man would want all over his body, if they
didn't happen to belong to his best friend. He was
a pro at ignoring that truth. "But I bet we can make
everyone believe you are."

She rolled her eyes. "Half the world already does."

"Then let's tell them all we are. It won't hurt anyone."

"How can it not? It'll be a lie. Our families aren't
going to believe that I up and changed grooms…"
Deep sadness filled her eyes. "Or maybe they would.
They won't believe it with you, though."

He cocked an eyebrow. "If I roll into town with hearts in my eyes, claiming that Jason dumping you was the catalyst for me finally seeing you're the woman of my dreams, people will believe it."

"Exactly, *lying*."

"It *won't* be a lie. *DIY I Do* will get a beautiful, real Christmas wedding. Our families will believe I was the spontaneous one this time, proposing to you because I love you. None of that is *technically* a lie…"

"Splitting hairs." She sighed. "But between being a relationship failure *and* going into debt and losing my shop, or marrying you and just being a relationship failure? The second is preferable."

He lifted a corner of his mouth. "I'm glad to be such an irresistible proposition."

She grinned, a hint of her usual ebullient self finally settling into place and staying put.

He took the twist tie off the bag of gummy bears, twisted it into a ring and presented it with a flourish.

"Be my bride, Beatrix Halloran?"

Her smile made him feel like the twist of paper and wire was platinum and diamonds. "I will."

"Bea, we're at the gate."

Mmm, Brody was a prime candidate for voicing a GPS app. Low and soothing but leaving no question he was in control of the situation. Even so, she wanted silence right now, not a location report.

"I know, I know," she complained. "Taking off soon. I won't sleep long. Promise. Just need a little nap." She tried to slide back into the darkness. Every hour of sleep she'd missed the night before was a brick weighing down her eyelids. Damn it, not time to wake up.

"Wrong gate." He chuckled. "We took off, flew and landed. It's showtime."

"No, it's naptime."

The plane's mechanical hum filled her ears—an aural hug. She tightened her two-handed grip around the biceps she was using as a comfort item. Sweet, sweet sleep, finally escaping the whirl of the last eighteen hours. Her pillow was too hard, but it was warm and covered in soft wool.

Brody didn't skimp when it came to his sweater yarn.

Gentle fingers teased her cheek. "We're *in Montana.*"

She jolted upright, opening her eyes. "What? You let me sleep the whole flight?"

He winced and peeled her clenched hands from around his upper arm. "Didn't exactly have a choice. You were out so hard, you didn't even revive when the flight attendant offered the classy snacks."

She groaned. "My inaugural first-class flight and I didn't even get a glass of champagne? Can I even say I flew it? I'm essentially still a first-class virgin!"

Someone snickered in the row behind them.

Her cheeks heated like an electrical outlet on the verge of shorting.

"First-class virgin is something else entirely," Brody said, cracking up.

A stern-faced flight attendant materialized in the aisle. Her name tag read Hilary. White with tanned skin that hinted at years of layovers in tropical places, she was a good six feet tall and polished to a marble shine. God, so put together. *Hilary* would never get dumped by her partner and need her best friend to step in and save her ass.

"I'm afraid *that* is against airplane regulations, even for the newly engaged," Hilary informed them.

Bea couldn't tell if the woman was serious or had a remarkable deadpan. Also, how did she know about the engagement? Bea shot Brody a questioning look.

He cocked an eyebrow as he packed away his ever-present knitting—his go-to for whenever he had time to kill. "What, you thought I was going to keep it a secret that you finally said yes? *I* wanted the champagne."

She harrumphed and then smiled an apology at the flight attendant. "Sorry if I disturbed anyone just now. I'm just sad I missed the refreshments."

Not the mile-high club, and especially not with Brody.

"*Refreshment* is just a fancy word for snack, after all." After giving Brody an obvious once-over with smoky-lidded eyes, Hilary sauntered back up the aisle.

He jammed his e-reader in the messenger bag he'd brought on board, not seeming to notice Hilary had just checked him out like an express-status library book. He rarely did.

Handy for those rare moments when attraction sneaked past her willpower, warming her straight through. He always seemed to miss the brief moments of weakness. And she never regretted putting up a shield to block out those feelings. He wouldn't be anyone's romantic dream, especially not hers. Keeping him as a friend was worth ignoring every cut muscle, every instance her heart wanted to melt at his smile, every suspicion she'd never fall in love with someone who understood her the way he did.

Not that she'd be falling in love with anyone while she was temporarily married to Brody. God, how were they going to explain this?

She poked his side. "Brody, we were supposed to use the flight to make up the rest of our story."

"We'll use the car ride to figure it out." He straightened, adjusted his seat belt and then leaned over to kiss her forehead.

Jeez, did he invest in ChapStick or something? His lips were the softest.

Which is not *the point.*

"What was that for?" she said, unable to stop her fingers from drifting to the place his mouth had been.

"We have forty minutes to get used to the kind of affection people expect out of an engaged couple. I figured we should start now."

"Well, warn a girl."

The imprint of his lips tingled on her forehead

the entire walk to baggage claim and while they waited for her mountain of suitcases and boxes in the bright wood-raftered space. Christmas elves had already visited to decorate, despite it not yet being Thanksgiving. Evergreen swags and bright red bows swathed the stone facades of the pillars.

Bea's stack of boxes and suitcases was a thousand times less festive, full of wasted dreams and unusable wedding paraphernalia. Frustration rising, she waved a hand at it. "Half that stuff isn't going to work for you and me. It was to appease Jason's mom, and no one's going to believe that it's what you and I want."

Brody rubbed her shoulder, his brown eyes confident. "We'll figure it out. I'll make a list in the car."

"I wish lists were halfway as comforting for me as they are for you," she said. Though necessary, all lists brought was the anxiety that she'd inevitably forget something, no matter how diligently she tried to check things off. "Are our families really going to believe that Jason and I have been broken up for more than a day? I mean, I've been talking to Emma about the wedding plans all week."

"So, we tell them we were covering it up because we wanted to talk to them in person."

Sounded weak to her ears, but maybe that, combined with Brody's promised story that her breakup with Jason was what finally made him realize he loved her, would convince someone who didn't know the truth.

It was worth trying. She didn't want to loop her family into her mess any more than she had to.

"We'd better be convincing." She stared at the clattering conveyor belt, willing her last suitcase to appear so they could get this over with. "I don't want to tell them and force them into lying to the production team on our behalf. The fewer people aware of the sham, the better."

He lifted her hand to his lips.

Yup, just as soft there as on her forehead.

"We're comfortable being affectionate. Ramp that up a little, and we'll be fine."

"What about an engagement story? And a ring! We don't have a ring—"

"We can rip into a store before we leave Bozeman." The corner of his mouth tilted. "I'll buy you something better than that skating rink Jason picked out. Something that doesn't scrape your flower petals."

Ugh, her old engagement ring *had* been a hazard while she worked with arrangements. She'd happily left it behind.

She rubbed her eyes, still foggy after her nap. She needed to pass out for a full day to make up for her packing all-nighter. "Okay. We'll pick up the bags, get our rental car and then have forty-five minutes to get our story straight."

"You bet, sleepyhead. If we plan fast, you might even catch another short nap."

"Ugh, knowing the emails the show's PA sent me,

we'll barely get time to breathe this week, let alone sleep."

"Makes for quite the wedding."

"Yeah." And this man... He was doing so much to salvage her pride, to facilitate her dreams. She took him in, casually slinging boxes onto two carts like their lives weren't about to undergo a massive change, even if temporarily. She laid a hand on his, forcing him to pause in his task. "Thank you, Brody."

"Of course." His tone was casual. His smile, too, flickering with humor at the corners. That serious gaze, though, not so much.

He knew this wasn't a small thing. Not the act of marriage, not the fact he was willing to undertake it with her for some rather unconventional reasons. His silent acknowledgment that their plan was nowhere near small potatoes eased the guilt of pulling him into her chaos.

He brushed a runaway curl off her forehead. "You look like a million bucks, Beatrix Halloran."

She wasn't sure how accurate he was with his "million bucks" compliment, but *he'd* certainly added an extra layer of shine when he'd gotten ready this morning. Instead of his usual athletic wear, he had on a crisp button-up shirt. Jeans hugged the ass and thighs that proved he did just as many squats as the rowers he coached. The guy had more than his fair share of genetic gifts and the work ethic to ensure he was still in elite shape. He was obviously practicing the engaged-couple affection he'd talked about—there was actual heat in his eyes—and *wow*, her bestie could be a smoke show when he put his mind to it.

Her cheeks warmed with embarrassment over drifting to a place she never let herself travel. *How about you put your mind to not looking at things you can't touch?*

They continued loading up the two carts. When finished, Brody's was stacked high enough to hide behind.

If only she could, instead of going out into the world.

"Here we go," she said under her breath, leading the way through the terminal toward the rental car counter.

"Hey, Bea?" he said, voice not betraying an ounce of the effort it had to be taking to push that cart.

"Yeah?"

"We got this. Hell, we might even enjoy ourselves."

The reminder settled into her soul, soothing her rattled nerves. They *did* usually manage to have fun, no matter what. It was one of the reasons she looked forward to seeing his face as much as possible. "Let's promise each other that. Priority number one—make this a fun time."

"You got it."

A streak of pink and denim exploded through a nearby door. "Surprise!"

Bea halted, just in time for a flurry of Emma, complete with a soundtrack of sisterly squeals, to bowl her over. Stopping short behind them, Brody muttered a curse.

"Bea!" Emma bounced on the toes of her pristine ankle boots and pushed up her purple-framed glasses. "I can't believe this is finally happening. Oh, my God, look at all the luggage. You're getting an arm workout, Ja— Brody?" She scanned around them, confusion widening her eyes. "Where's Jason?"

Brody rounded the side of the cart to stand with Bea. He nodded at her, as if to say, "Take it away, boss."

She glared back at him, trying to get across something like *Are you kidding me? I can't explain this to my sister because we don't have our story straight and she can read me like a nursery rhyme* in the matter of a second. Preventing said sister, of course, from reading any of the silent message.

"It's okay, sweetheart. We're here now," he said, and wow, he was impressive. Using an endearment he never used for her. Making it sound like it was a private comment but keeping his voice just loud enough for Emma to catch every syllable. "We can finally tell the truth."

The truth?

She barely held in a laugh.

"Bea, where's Jason?" Emma repeated, peering down the hall to the baggage carousels.

Time to rip off the proverbial bandage. Bea shuffled next to Brody and laced her fingers in his. "He's not coming."

Emma froze, except for her gaze bouncing between them faster than a ball at a Grand Slam tennis match. "I don't understand."

Bea held their joined hands up like they were standing on a podium and repeated her sister's "Surprise!" just in time to see the outside door slide open and the camera crew standing on the sidewalk. Her heart spun up into her throat. "Wait, you brought an entourage?"

"Didn't you want me to? What better scene is there than an airport greeting?" Blinking, Emma turned so that she was facing away from the door. "Except, you know, when my sister doesn't *bring her fiancé*."

"I did. I—" Two of the show people broke off from the group and started walking toward them. "Damn it! Emma, lend me your engagement ring."

"What?"

"Your ring! I need to borrow it," she said, trying not to move her lips.

"Where's yours?"

"In Seattle." *In Jason's blender, waiting for the next time he makes a smoothie.* "Your ring. *Please.* I'll get it back to you later tonight."

"No. My engagement ring is an emerald, remember? It's too distinctive." Yanking a yellow-gold band crowned with five small diamonds off her right hand, Emma thrust it at Bea. "This is Luke and Brody's grandma's anniversary band. If you need a ring, wear this."

She took the pretty piece of Emerson family history. Being an heirloom, it made more sense for her to wear it than to borrow Emma's. *Or you're completely dishonoring the love between Brody's grandparents.*

Ugh. That sat so wrong, but she didn't know what else to do. She had just enough time to slide it on her left hand and greet the approaching duo with her best attempt at gracious excitement.

"And here's the happy couple!" The voice was Christmas-bells-a-ringing wrapped up in hot chocolate warmth.

Rashida Martinez, host extraordinaire and one of the show's producers, sidled up to them, medium brown cheeks tinged with rose. She wore black jeans, lace-up ankle boots and a cashmere sweater that looked soft enough to line a baby's bassinet. A sound tech trailed behind her, carrying three clip-on microphones.

Right. They'd be wearing those for the next week. *No more thinking out loud for me.*

Rashida stuck out her hand. "Bea, so good to see you." Her Southern roots drew out her words. "We couldn't secure permits for filming in the airport today, so we'll need to set up a greeting shot on the sidewalk. Make it look spontaneous."

"But I'm—" Bea looked down at her leggings and sneakers. "I was planning to wear something nicer for my first appearance." And who knew if there would even be an appearance if the production team didn't agree to the fiancé switch.

"Don't you worry about that. You look approachable. And heaven knows Jason will look like he stepped off a J.Crew billboard. Is he still at baggage claim? Or in the washroom? We'll get the three of you miked up and—" She squinted at Brody and then down at his fingers laced through Bea's. "Wait. You must be Brody. The best man. Bride's man, that is. Or man of honor. Whatever term you settled on. But holding hands isn't going to fly. I'm not here to judge whatever works for you, but my viewership isn't going to like even a hint of a love triangle to complicate your big romance, Bea."

Rashida had met Jason, not only in the audition and background check process but during a day of filming they'd done in Seattle to establish their engagement story. Rashida's reputation for being a delight was one of the reasons Bea had been excited to sign up for *DIY I Do*. A coworker from her theme park days had gone on to do things with StreamFlix and swore up and down that Rashida was dedicated to her project and wanted to put out a quality product. She wouldn't screw Bea over with misrepresentation or false drama.

I'm the one screwing her *over. With* real *drama.*

Bea forced a smile, but no way would Rashida be fooled. No person trained to deal with people in Hollywood would miss the stiffness in Bea's lips. "Good to see you, too, Rashida. It's…well, it's not a love triangle. We need to run something by you. Before we get those microphones on." She glanced around the busy airport. "Somewhere private, though?"

"Where is your groom, Bea?" Rashida said.

"You're looking at him," Brody cut in. One of his wide palms slid along Bea's back. The other reached out to shake Rashida's. "Also, at the luckiest man in Montana."

The host looked puzzled as anything. "I'm sorry, what?"

Brody slid a palm along Bea's cheek.

He looked a mix of recalcitrant and eager and… infatuated? His mouth lowered.

Was he going to *kiss* her?

Once or twice, it had crossed her mind that he'd be worth kissing. Usually after a few drinks lowered her good sense and inhibitions. *"Brody—"*

"She wants big romance, Sparks." The bossy whisper tickled her ear. His lips landed on her cheek.

She shivered.

He'd kissed her cheek a hundred times before. Tiny pecks of *hello* or *goodbye* or *thank you for coming to Brazil to watch me win Olympic gold.* This one had more meaning behind it. Came with the spirit of *I'm trying to appease my fiancée.*

Rashida held up a hand. "I do not understand. *Jason* is the groom, and I have six hours of footage to prove it."

Between Rashida's sharp gaze and the horror dawning in Emma's expression, Bea could swear that the stone posts and wooden beams were angling in toward her, ready to collapse on her at any minute. Much like her poorly constructed story.

"The footage—can we reshoot it?" she asked.

"Reshoot it?"

The host said it like Bea was asking to move the wedding to the surface of the moon.

Squaring her shoulders, she nodded. "We'll need to do something. The footage you have won't work. Jason and I broke up a couple of weeks ago. Which was what I needed—exactly what I needed—to realize I was in love with Brody."

Chapter Three

The sidewalk in front of the airport wasn't all that better a location to continue her explanation than the middle of the airport, but Bea would at least take the fresh air.

Rashida stood with her pink-tipped fingers gripping her hips, seemingly impervious to the cold. "This all sounds like a bad reality TV episode."

"Uh…" Brody stared at her.

"I make *good* reality TV."

"And we want to be a part of that," Bea said, suppressing a shiver. She hadn't traveled with a coat—figured she could walk from the terminal to the rental car in her yoga hoodie.

The drag of a zipper rang out and a thin but cozy teal puffer jacket landed on her shoulders.

"No need to freeze, Sparks," Brody murmured, standing behind her and rubbing her upper arms with his strong hands.

Her knee-jerk reaction was to slough off the gesture, but that wouldn't paint a picture of a head-over-heels couple. She snuggled into the warmth and scooched a step backward so she was fully in his embrace.

Rashida's face scrunched in disbelief. "So let me get this straight—"

"Please, let's," Emma added under her breath, her face a veritable storm cloud.

"You broke up with Jason and immediately got engaged to someone else?" Rashida said.

"To my best friend." Bea tried to sound confident.

"Bea." Her sister's reprimand was a gunshot across the parking lot.

She kept her eyes on the host. If she didn't look at Emma, she wouldn't risk giving away the truth with an inadvertent expression.

"You weren't marrying your best friend?" Rashida asked. Snickers came from the small crew. She hushed them with a wave of her hand.

"I wasn't," she admitted. It seemed best to be as honest as she could, and she had some major truths to reckon with when it came to why she'd settled on the idea of marrying someone who didn't love every part of her. "Jason turned out not to be the one."

Emma squeaked. Bea risked a fleeting glare, willing her to be patient.

"Evidently," Rashida said dryly.

"You know when you let go of something that's just not right for you?" Bea said carefully, the idea spinning as she spoke. "And you can finally see what's right in front of you? I let go of Jason, and I…" She twisted partway to lock eyes with the man at her back. Her rock. If this gambit changed their relationship, she'd never forgive herself. "I saw Brody," she finished.

"And I finally let myself see Bea," he added.

A sigh came from her sister. "I *knew* you two would eventually end up together. Why didn't you tell me?"

Emma had clearly gone from doubtful to convinced. Maybe *too* convinced. Bea's sister was a die-hard romantic. Though Brody's soft, affectionate smile *would* be believable to the uninitiated.

Enough to convince Rashida—and an audience?

The host crossed her arms. "*DIY I Do* isn't about scandalous breakups and makeups and spontaneous matches. I staked my reputation on creating a show that doesn't need to be salacious to get a viewership. This is not the story I signed you on to tell. Bea, you applied as an opposites-attract trope. A buttoned-up, bemused groom and his free-spirited, creative bride. The wedding businesses and a mountain aesthetic that'll have people thinking of that 'Snow' song in *White Christmas*."

"I know this isn't what you expected." Bea fixed Rashida with an imploring look. "Which is why we stalled in filling you in. Our families, too. We wanted to talk to them in person. Would you be willing to tell our story, though? Some of what you loved is still intact. Brody's not buttoned-up, but I'm sure he could pretend bemusement. And friends to lovers is a thing, right?"

Rashida's expression sharpened. "If I'm going to create the mood this show is known for, he can't pretend anything."

Bea's stomach twisted. "I didn't mean it like that. Just that I tend to go down rabbit holes, and Brody's always the one who finds it amusing instead of annoying." She kept her gaze off her sister, who was always getting frustrated by Bea's shifting priorities. "I don't think 'bemused' will be a stretch for him."

"It's more than that," Rashida said. "It's having an authentic relationship and a poignant story for the viewers. They want true love, a couple who will obviously be together forever."

"We will be," Brody said, sliding his arm around Bea's shoulders.

Again, that intent.

Again, a shiver Bea wasn't used to.

Perfect rose-brown lips pressed into a firm line. Rashida's gaze danced from Brody's hand on Bea's shoulder to Bea's hands—oh, crap, she was fidgeting with the borrowed ring—to Emma's face.

Emma's mouth turned up in a wobbly smile. "And

hey, there's the whole sisters-marrying-their-child-hood-neighbors angle, too. With Luke and I being together, and now Brody and Bea."

"Cousins, no less," Brody said. His grip tensed on Bea's shoulder. "I mean, Luke and I are cousins, not that any cousins are getting married."

Another snort from a crew member.

"Y'all are something else," Rashida said. "So. Friends to lovers. Instalove." She sighed. "I just don't know."

"It's not instalove." Brody brought one of Bea's hands to his lips like he'd done while they waited at baggage claim. "Not for me, anyway. I've loved Bea since she was ten. She showed up on my doorstep with a treasure map, intent on distracting me from the loss of my dad. Little did I know at the time that the real treasure was her."

Bea's breath caught. The warmth of his breath on her knuckles was a sensation she'd never anticipated enjoying, but damn, she didn't want it to end. He had a way of taking the truth and tying it up with their fabricated relationship until it sounded real.

"He was a couple grades ahead of me. We were neighbors. After his dad died in Afghanistan, I missed seeing Brody happy on the bus ride to school," she added.

"Almost childhood sweethearts," Rashida mused.

"Slap whatever label on us you like," he said. "As long as I get to marry Bea, I'm getting everything I'll ever need."

No one had ever said that about her before. Not even Jason.

But the man saying it now would never truly mean it.

Longing tugged at her heart. She shoved it away. That was the grief of a breakup talking—proof she needed time to be by herself before she considered another relationship. And whenever she was ready to fall in love again, it wouldn't be with someone who wasn't capable of fully loving her back.

Brody had stepped up when it mattered, though, and was giving her what he could. And because of that, she would be able to follow through on the wedding and wouldn't lose her shop. And just as important, her choices wouldn't harm her family.

"Let us show you," Bea said.

Almost begged, really.

Rashida crossed her arms. "We have to scrap all the pre-footage. Viewers expect to see a picture of your hometown. We don't have the budget to go back to Seattle to film your life there."

Bea swallowed. *Life?* Try *lives*. They were completely separate, still. How were they going to fake *together*? "Sutter Creek is our hometown, really. We can show you around here. The lake where Brody started rowing…" Crap, that was more about him alone. What else—what things where they were together? "Uh, the bakery where I worked part-time, and he ate his weight in donuts? And the ranch! I taught him how to ride a horse."

Rashida's smile was wishy-washy.

"Or we could play up Christmas traditions. I'm sure there's something we could decorate, or we could talk about the lodge's Christmas festival. We always helped out with that in our teens."

"We could have them decorate a tree," Rashida's PA threw out.

"Yes!" Emma said. "We have tons of family ornaments. So does Brody's grandfather. Or does your mom have anything of yours, Brody?"

He paled a little. "Uh…"

Damn it. "Where would we decorate, though?" Bea said. "It would be weird to have us putting up a tree together anywhere but, uh, our town house. And it's not like we've decorated a tree together before. It isn't a tradition of ours. Yet." It wasn't a tradition of Brody's at all. She was fairly sure the last time he and his mom had a tree was before his dad died.

His pained expression aligned with her guess. "I like the rowing idea better. Or the barn."

"We're not doing an activity that isn't something you would normally do," Rashida said. "We're not on board with setting up fake shots."

Bea felt the blood rush from her face.

"Today was supposed to be for setup, planning, rehearsals, getting you and *Jason* firm on the schedule." Rashida's head shake sent her sleek ponytail swinging. "We'll have to cut that down and squeeze in some extra B-roll and interviews."

Did that mean she was going along with this?

Bea let out a breath big enough to buffet the small plane taking off on the nearby runway. Wow. They were going to get the chance to salvage the plan. She grinned up at Brody.

He kissed her cheek again and then smiled at Rashida. "Tell us where to be, and we'll be there."

"I can't decide who's glaring at me more—that horse or my sister."

Brody laughed and nuzzled the side of Bea's face.

"Yeah, that's definitely what's making Nora glower," she said.

"Good," he said.

There was something wholly fulfilling about riling Nora, the eldest Halloran sibling. Given Brody was the captain of Team Bea, his ultraprotective head had reared over the years when her siblings gave her a hard time for marching to her own beat. He'd been testing Nora's patience for the last ten minutes while the crew tested lighting. Every time he touched Bea, Nora let out a small growl. Her reaction made putting on a show for the film crew that much more rewarding.

It feels pretty damn rewarding, Nora or no.

Film crew or no, for that matter.

Being physically near Bea was no hardship.

Probably something that should've made him nervous, but it was going to mean getting to the finish line with less effort, so he was going to focus on that.

Brody shuffled even closer, bumping Bea's knees

with his thighs. She was perched on the top rail of a low stall in the least-used barn on the RG Ranch, ankles hooked around the next rail down. Her hands gripped the wood next to her hips. One stall over, Nora held the lead of her palomino, who'd been one of the horses moved from the main barn to this one in case Rashida decided she wanted footage of Bea and Brody riding.

"I can't speak for the horse, but I don't think Nora approves," he said quietly. They weren't miked, so it was the first chance they'd had to talk without someone listening in since Emma had mobbed them in the airport.

"Yeah, she made a snide comment about me having to follow through, or else my parents would have to clean up my mess again and they can't afford it."

Christ. Everyone would benefit from chilling out a little—he and Bea had this. He chanced a glance at Nora, who was staring at them with fire in her eyes.

"Not that you were planning on asking them for help, but she figures your parents' finances are that tight?"

She frowned. "The ranch's bottom line, yeah. It's no secret they're struggling. And you know Nora— she always assumes they'll bail me out, especially since they helped me after the ice cream truck."

"All the more reason to make sure this works." He traced a finger along the delicate edge of her jaw.

A grumble floated over from the paddock.

"If this is how Nora's reacting, what the hell is my

mom going to think?" Bea whispered back. "I really wish we'd had time to talk to her."

With all the speed of getting Rashida to agree, facing a barrage of questions from Emma and Luke and then changing into barn-appropriate clothes before driving to the ranch to start filming, Bea hadn't gotten the chance to talk to her parents in person.

"We'll head over to the main house as soon as we're done here," he promised.

"No, I'm going to need to make a hundred and fifty wedding favors." She made a face. "Cellophane bags of these Christmas-scented essential oils Jason's mom loved. Not my thing at all."

"Hey." He tapped a finger to her nose and lifted his eyebrows. "It's our wedding. Let's brainstorm something different."

Her brow furrowed. "Like what?"

"We'll cobble something together. For now, let's pret—"

Bea poked him in the gut, cutting off the word.

"Good call. Not even when the mics are off. What I meant was, for now, let's show them how we're madly in love."

"Madly in love?" Green eyes glinted with determination. Her hands looped around the back of his neck.

"You know it." It was impossible to ignore the camera rolling, capturing what was supposed to be B-roll footage of them in the barn, "canoodling" as Rashida had instructed. She wanted shots of them laughing, like a live-action engagement session. "I think we're supposed to look relaxed, at minimum."

"So, flirt with me, *fiancé*."

He braced his hands on the rail next to her hips and leaned to one of her ears. She smelled a little like flowers. Fresh and clean cutting through the funk of dust and hay. "Want to know something about yourself that I've never told you?"

"That sounds ominous."

"No, it's not. It's just something I've noticed. You know how some people smell the same their whole lives?"

"Sure." She tilted her head a little and her nose bumped the hairline behind his ear. "Doesn't everyone?"

"Not you." He risked covering her hands with his. "I mean, you always have this fresh sunshine thing going on, but every time you head down a new path, you take on a hint of something different."

Her smile faltered. "Oh…"

"No, it's a good thing. Always something new to discover. When you were in Orlando, it was sweet. Cotton candy and confectioners' sugar."

"Internalizing all that saccharine princess messaging, I guess," she said.

Her fingers threaded into the hair at the back of his head, and one of her thumbs traced from his earlobe down his jaw. He shivered. Did she know that was one of his erogenous zones? Had he mentioned that at one point? He didn't think the point of this was to actually turn each other on, but he supposed it *would* be more convincing if they managed to, just a little.

Turning his head, he retaliated with a slow kiss to her temple.

Her hands tightened on the back of his neck.

"In Costa Rica, it was papaya," he said.

"Well, that was just my sunscreen. I had to bathe in the stuff to make sure I didn't burn."

He chuckled. "The number of times you've slapped sun protection on me—"

"You get double the sun reflecting off the water." She scooted her hands out from his hair and brought her fingertips to the outer corners of his eyes. "Gotta guard against premature lines and melanoma."

"So you keep telling me."

She huffed out a sigh and settled her palms on his shoulders. "Men always look hot with crow's-feet, anyway." Another sigh. "Something tells me they don't want us talking about skin aging right now."

"They're not recording what we're saying. All they care about is that we look intimate."

Her throat bobbed. "Right."

One of her hands slid up his shoulder to the side of his neck. It was shaking a bit.

It took everything he had not to start shaking himself.

"I thought we were trying to relax," he said, keeping his voice as low as he could.

He lifted her other hand and ran a thumb along the ring on her fourth finger. Kinda wild, having her wear his grandma's ring. Five diamonds, one for each decade his grandparents had been married. It somehow looked exactly right on Bea's hand.

"Fits perfectly," he rasped.

"I feel terrible wearing it. Like I'm making a mockery of what your grandparents had."

"It's just a bunch of stones, Bea. And it looks pretty on your finger."

One of the horses nickered. A camera operator coughed. Two of the PAs were chatting about what they felt was paltry nightlife in Sutter Creek. The ten other humans buzzing around the barn were an excellent reminder of why his best friend's hand was touching his neck in a way she'd never done before. He and Bea were here for the cameras.

"How intimate do you think they'll want us to be?" he whispered.

Eyes wide, she shifted and wobbled. One of her legs slipped free from where she'd hooked it. She pitched backward with a shriek.

In lurching to catch her, his knees hit the middle fence rail. His hands absorbed her weight, shifting her upright. His heart beat a tattoo against his ribs.

"Oh, my God," she said, panting. "You and your athlete's reflexes."

"Jeez, Bea. That would have been a hard landing."

Nodding against his chest, she heaved in a breath.

He spread his fingers along her waist, wanting her to feel secure, safe.

Nothing about getting married and then quietly annulling our union is safe.

And explaining their split wouldn't be easy. He fully intended to take the blame and didn't like the idea of their families being disappointed with him for not being able to commit. But being honest now and breaking Bea's contract with StreamFlix would be worse.

He swallowed. He needed to be positive. Stay focused. Put on a bit of a show for the show. Then once in Seattle, after they were married, they could go back to their normal relationship, and this would be something they'd laugh about in secret. One more inside joke their friends would give them grief about having… Except they'd probably need to keep all that to themselves, too. For the sake of the producers not finding out, it would be best to convince their friends it was real.

"You okay there, Bea?" the director, a middle-aged white guy named Mark Evans, called out.

"Yeah, I'm fine," she said, though she still sounded shaky.

"Y'all look adorable," Rashida said, standing next to Mark, a studious expression on her face. "Don't be afraid to shake on a hint of spice for the tape."

Bea looped her hands around Brody's waist and brought their faces close. "How spicy is *spicy*, Rashida?"

"Kissing's fine. Anything you'd label *tender*. But

nothing that would make your grandmother blush," the producer said.

A gasp came from the back of the barn, followed by low curses from both Bea and Nora.

He turned his head to see what had caught their attention.

Oh, crap. Bea's mom, Georgie. Her livid expression fixated on Brody's hands.

It took everything he had to keep playing the role, not to pull away.

"Bea. *Brody.* I think before you worry about what Nana and Poppy have to say, you'll need to worry about your father and me."

Chapter Four

Noise erupted around Bea, filling the barn and startling the horses—Brody's soft curse, Nora's sharper one, someone yelling "cut."

None of it was as loud as her mother's silence. Georgie Halloran was smoldering like a bed of hot coals—a temper Bea needed to tamp out before it lit her farce on fire.

"Mom," Bea yelped, resisting the impulse to pull away from Brody. This wasn't tenth grade, and she hadn't just been caught making out behind the hay bales with the captain of the boys' hockey team. She and Brody were getting married, even if there wouldn't be any cuddling or kissing once they weren't in the public eye.

We're not doing anything wrong.
Not really.

She slid from the fence and casually disentangled herself from Brody. Like a person would from a lover, not like someone ashamed of what they were doing. The comforting smells of hay, dirt and animals washed over her. She'd never call herself a rancher or a farm girl—that was Nora's realm, not hers—but the remnants of her childhood still centered her, even with the reminder that she'd never quite fit.

And going by the hurt and anger in her mom's blue eyes, Bea needed all the centering she could get.

She shot an apologetic look at Rashida. "Our whole 'tell them in person' plan? Well, I haven't had time to inform my mom yet."

Rashida frowned but waved at Bea in a clear gesture to take a quick break.

"By all means, don't let me interrupt," Georgie called across the barn.

"Except you did interrupt," Bea muttered, taking Brody's hand and tugging him along, making her way past the crew. Chatter and whispers accompanied her quick strides. A whole lot of "Even her mom didn't know about the change in groom?"

She cringed.

Yeah, I'm confused about the change in groom part, too.

Not the "Jason dumping her" part. That couldn't have been easier to understand, and so obviously a blessing in disguise. But she still wasn't sure how she'd gone from dumped to vamping on a fence for a camera with a brand-new, fake-as-hell fiancé.

Instead of letting on how it was surreal to be walking hand in hand with her best friend, she doubled down, lifting their joined hands and holding them to her cheek.

His fingers flexed in hers, but his gaze stayed on her mom as they came to a halt a few feet from where she stood in the wide barn doorway, ten or so feet from anyone involved in filming. In her worn-out Seahawks cap and lined denim jacket, Georgie looked like she'd just come in off the range.

And her jaw hung lower than if she'd returned from the fields to discover an asteroid had taken out the barn.

Bea gave her a quick hug but only got a shocked half squeeze in return.

"We're trying to catch up on filming, Mom," she said. "Could we come to the house and explain when we're done?"

"No. If you're going to bring a crowd into my barn, you're going to tell me why, now. I don't understand. This…" Georgie waved a hand at Bea and Brody. Her gaze flicked to the crew behind them. "Them."

"Nora okayed 'them,'" she said, making finger quotes with her free hand. "As for 'this,' uh… Surprise?"

"Honestly, Georgie?" Brody said, leaning in. "It's a surprise for us, too."

All he got in response was a miffed squeak.

Bea leaned into Brody's arm. The knit of his sweater brushed her cheek. Soft wool over hard muscle. Intricate little stitches made with hand-spun sock-weight yarn he'd picked up at a crafting store on a last-minute trip they'd taken to New York City years ago. God, he'd taken forever in that store. And he'd knit the golden-brown cardigan while training for his last Olympics. She'd never bothered to tell him that some of the flecks matched his eyes, but somehow, now, it seemed like an important detail.

Focus, Bea. "How does a person explain love, Mom?"

"Fairly easily, Beatrix." Thank God she was at least keeping her voice down. "You meet someone. Get to know them. Enjoy their company and their jokes and looking at their face. Decide your goals for your lives are similar, or at least complementary. Decide you want to build a life together."

Bea winked at Brody. "And we've done all those things."

Georgie's face darkened. "This isn't what broke up you and Jason, was it? You didn't—"

"Mom!" Bea made a shushing motion with her hand. "No. God, no. Jason was the one..." She darted a glance over her shoulder at Rashida, who was shuffling in place, impatient as a toddler at a candy buffet. "Look, there's more of a story to tell, but can we do it later? We're already needing to play catch-up, make up for lost footage."

"Because you changed grooms." Georgie cleared her throat. "You've always been my honeybee, my flit-from-flower-to-flower child, but this—"

"Except this isn't—"

Brody nudged her with an elbow.

Not to mention her sister's eyes burning into her back like a cattle brand. Nora's words from earlier, when they'd arrived in a flurry and needed her co-operation to get set up for impromptu filming, rang in her head. *This better be real, and you better follow through. Our parents will always bail you out. But this time, it might put us under.*

"Give it a few minutes, Georgie. It'll make sense, I promise. This is…" He put on a smile Bea had seen many a time. The one he wore when a race official was hanging a gold medal around his neck. "It's everything I've ever wanted." The smile turned bashful. "*Bea* is everything I've ever wanted. And we've waited too long to be apart any longer."

Kaitlin, the production assistant who had been examining Bea and Brody like she was assessing them for the front page of a tabloid, hurried over. "You have one more minute."

Bea's mom crossed her arms.

"You probably have more than a minute's worth of questions," Bea said lightly.

A curt nod.

She glanced at the crew. Off in the distance, Nora was still fussing over her horse.

"Nora!" She waved her sister over.

Shockingly, Nora obliged.

"Can you fill Mom in on anything I left out?" Bea asked.

"Fill Mom in?"

She cocked a brow. "On everything we talked about when we arrived."

"Why would you tell Nora before your *mother*?" Georgie whispered.

"We ran into some snags, and—"

"It's a long story," Nora cut in, taking their mom by the shoulders and shuttling her away, shooting Bea a glare.

For once, she didn't mind her sibling stepping into the bossy big sister role. If Nora was worried about their parents' finances, then she could help with the farce, even if she didn't know it was a farce.

But Georgie—she'd looked so hurt.

Bea squeezed Brody's hand and let go. "I'll be back in ten seconds." She jogged after the retreating pair.

"Mom!" she said. "Wait."

Georgie spun on a boot heel. "What?"

"We're making favors after we finish up here. Do you want to help with that?"

"Favors. For your *wedding*. To a person I didn't know you were engaged to." Her mom managed to spit those words out like they were sour milk. "You'd better handle this one on your own. I need some time to process."

"Okay."

She turned, feeling small.

Only Brody's smile buoyed her enough to walk back onto the makeshift set.

Brody picked up one of the carefully lined-up bottles of scented oil. While most of the small crew had been at the barn, a few had remained behind to set up for the craft session. Cellophane bags, stacks of aromatherapy sticks, scented oils and empty bottles lined a long table. He took a sniff of the small vial. "Smells like Christmas dessert on a yacht. Or maybe in the Hamptons."

Bea laughed. "This is what I was telling you."

This was supposed to be her wedding favor? How had she agreed to that? It was the least Bea-like smell he could think of. "It in no way makes me think of us."

She got in close, a comforting whiff of her sunny-day scent catching him in the chest. "And for people to believe this, we have to make it personal."

"Gotta get creative." Despite the fact the last-minute change would tick off the production crew. He didn't see using any of the prepared items, but so far, there wasn't an idea to replace it.

They couldn't ask for a better setting to get their thinking caps on. The great hall of the Moosehorn River Lodge was a downright work of art, from the evergreen swags and holly bundles Emma had hung up earlier than normal for the sake of filming to the pristine cream paint on the walls and rustic-but-intricate woodwork on the loft railings and stair-well. The staircase, crafted by Alejandra, Bea and Emma's talented new sister-in-law, resembled bare forest branches, spiraling from the loft above clear through the dining area and down to the lounge and coffee bar on the floor below. The massive structure suited the equally expansive room's soaring ceilings and windows. Sound and lighting techs and camera operators were busy poring over angles and power outlets and other technical decisions.

Bea paced in front of Brody, the glittery shoes she'd shown him over their video chat last night clicking on the artisan-milled flooring. She'd changed when they got back from filming in the barn. She'd paired the heels with shiny, dark red leggings, a long T-shirt and a velvet blazer. Her white-blond curls were their usual curated mess.

He took in her outfit's color palette, along with the holiday decor spritzing every available surface of the lodge's grand dining room. "Our favor needs to be more than personal—we need festive. Something more Christmassy than some vaguely plum pudding–scented oils in a jar."

She smirked. "Don't forget the sticks."

He picked two of them up and pretended to use them as knitting needles. "They're the right size for sock yarn but are too blunt on the ends to use."

Her gaze flicked from his hands to the box of to-be-discarded favors. "We're both crafty. We should be able to figure out something new." She glanced at the large clock hanging above the mantel—a significant improvement over the stuffed fish Emma had used her magic to wheedle his grandfather into hanging in his garage. "In ten minutes."

Raising his hands in an "easy, now" gesture, he said, "Beyond knitting, I'm not crafty. And any kind of yarn work would take too long. I mean, I guess there might be some sort of speedy crocheted ornament, but you know I can't crochet worth a damn." He'd leaned into his knitting-in-the-stands reputation over the years. Every regatta had long stretches of waiting, and working yarn around needles was meditative. Productive, too. He got a kick out of seeing people wear the things he'd made or being able to put some more elaborate pieces up for auction to raise funds for some of the charitable causes that asked for his support.

Bea picked up the sticks and then the glass jar, examining them. "A friend of mine once made ornaments by filling a glass ball with curled strips of her wedding invitation. It was pretty."

"Uh, we don't have a wedding invitation, Sparks."

Her chin jerked up, her eyes a little wide. "*Guests*, Brody. What are we going to do about guests? It'll look weird if we don't have any of your friends attend, or your side of the family."

"Hey." He stroked a hand down her cheek. So soft. Still on the chillier side from a couple hours in the barn. "Let's save that worry for after we finish the favors."

"Right." She groaned. "Don't let me forget."

Her long blink set off his worry-meter. He was a pro at detecting signs of Bea getting overwhelmed.

"Here." He pulled out his phone and pulled up the Notes app. "I'll start a list. Anytime you think of a thread that we can't drop, I'll make a note of it, and we'll check things off as best we can. As much as I know you'd like to be doing five things at once, we have to focus on one thing at a time."

"You're right." She held one of the bottles up to the light. "What if we repurposed them somehow?"

He tested the weight of one of the bottles. "Do you think these would be too heavy to hang on a tree?"

She frowned. "Maybe."

"Too bad. We could have done a message in a bottle."

"Cute." She grinned. "Or a treasure map."

"A treasure map?" His throat constricted. As much as it was the impetus for Bea's initial burst onto the stage of his life, the viewing public didn't need details on his dad's death. He and his mom had struggled through that pain enough over the years. "I don't know how much of that particular story I can parade in front of the camera, Bea. It's too connected to my dad, and that's my mom's and my business. It would hurt her to have it dissected by a bunch of strangers in their living rooms."

Her rosy cheeks paled a bit. "Of course. I'm sorry, I wasn't thinking."

"I'm fine."

"It would hurt you, too."

But it was easier to focus on his mom than deal with grief that never completely faded. "It won't be an issue. You were just spitballing, and you might be onto something with the treasure map. A way to use it as inspiration without me having to get into all the details. Rashida liked our rundown of all the places that mean something to us in town." He snapped his fingers. "What about a map of Sutter Creek?"

Inspiration brightened her expression. "A sketch. With our favorite haunts highlighted on it."

He rolled one of the bottles in his hand. "Inside these?"

"No, you're right. Those wouldn't hang well. But there are those actual ornaments that you can fill with stuff—" She waved a hand. "Not the right shape, though… Maybe jar lids."

"Like Mason jars?"

"Yes," she said, then shook her head. "I doubt we have time to collect them—"

"My grandfather still has my grandmother's old canning stuff in his garage. She used to stock up. Probably has hundreds of the rings."

She clapped her hands together. "I've got it. You get the rings. I'll work on the map."

"Bea." He stacked his hands on top of his head. "You aren't the only one who hasn't had the chance to talk to their family. I don't know what the hell I'm going to say to my grandfather."

She fixed those knowing green eyes on him. "Tell him what you need to, Brody. If you can't lie, don't."

"Lie about what?" came a woman's voice.

He and Bea both jumped. Brody scrambled for an answer to the question.

Kaitlin stood with her arms wrapped around a clipboard and an expression sharper than a tip on a straight-out-of-the-box pencil.

"We were contemplating softening the truth of how quickly we got together for Brody's grandpa," Bea said coolly. "He's traditional, you know?"

Kaitlin played with the tip of her long red pony-tail. "You're not the story we normally tell."

That jolted Brody from his stasis. He shuffled closer to Bea, put a hand on her shoulder and then kissed the top of her head. Her mess of curls tickled his nose. "But we're a good one, though."

The PA's pursed lips broadcast a clear *that remains to be seen.* "Good or not, it's time to put together these favors." She pointed to the meticulously organized table. "I have it all set out for you."

Bea winced. "About that. This design—it was meant to appease Jason's mom. Now that I'm freer to be me, I'm thinking of doing something else." She gave an explanation of how the maps and canning rings would fit together with hot glue.

"But we're organized to do *this*." Kaitlin's jaw jutted out.

"And if you give Brody and me a few more seconds, we'll be ready to do something that's authentic to us. I promise, it'll be super pretty."

"How is anything canning-related close to luxurious?"

"It'll be real. We can worry about luxurious with other things."

"And the time we'll lose while you run around collecting kitschy crap?" The PA's voice carried the edge of a person who'd had to make one too many last-minute changes today.

Brody nodded. "I get schedules. On regatta weekends, my life is structured down to the minute. Similar to you, I bet." Kaitlin's expression softened minutely. "And while we need to work within your structure, for sure, we need to remember that the magic won't happen unless things are truly about Bea and me."

"And a story that you're still not sold on, but I promise is amazing," Bea said.

"You need to talk to me about the magic," Rashida said, joining them from across the room. "Kaitlin's in charge of crossing off the lists. I'm the one that crafts the story." She grabbed a bottle of the oil, opened it and inhaled. Her nose wrinkled. "That smells like every holiday-season run-in I ever had with the Baton Rouge debutantes before I clawed my way west to Los Angeles. Not the vibe I get from either of you. Tell me this new concept of yours."

A half hour later, cameras were rolling. Stacks of pilfered canning paraphernalia and a glue gun littered the table, not nearly so neat as Kaitlin's initial organizational efforts.

Brody's fingers flew over strands of the skein of yarn he'd unearthed from his grandma's remaining stash. Not knitting—he was tasked with a hundred simple braids to wrap around the eventual seams of the canning rings—but up his alley, nonetheless.

Bea was busy hand-lettering a small map that would be one side of the ornament. Emma was busy running off duplicates of the other side—a circle marked with their names, their wedding date and personalized icons of a bee on a flower and a knitting needle crossed with an oar that Bea had sketched a few minutes ago.

He peered over his fiancée's shoulder, examining her careful pen work over a basic line drawing of a few of Sutter Creek's main streets. She'd starred and lettered their high school and the Raffertys' bakery and was working on the RG Ranch brand.

"This is sweet stuff, you two," Rashida said, turning on her hosting shine. "Tell me about this map."

"It's some of our meaningful places." Bea held her sketch up for the camera. "Brody and I may live in Seattle, but Sutter Creek is a part of our souls."

No lies there. "That hometown nostalgia," he added. "There's barely a memory I have that doesn't include Bea."

The pretty map flowing out of her pen onto crisp cardstock proved his point. Life before his dad died, before Bea turned up on his porch with her winsome smile and her treasure map, was a hazy mix of learning to fly-fish in the river, his dad teaching him to swim and row in their inflatable dinghy, his mom's smile. God, he missed that smile.

Sure, she'd physically gone through the motions during his teen years. He'd held her together as best he could. But even his college successes and international medals had only earned a faded facsimile of the joy they'd had before that IED had blown up not just his dad's convoy, but all their lives. She'd moved from the lodge property into town after Brody graduated. Though he saw her every chance he got, he always felt like he was clawing through layers of scar tissue when he visited her.

Hers and his both.

A lump filled his throat, and he realized he'd stopped braiding.

Bea was chattering away, something about the history of the lodge as she lettered the lodge's old name next to an intricate doodle of a fishing fly.

He let her ramble, trying to swallow down the grief that insisted on washing over him when he least expected it.

All those points on the map, the connections tying them together…

He wasn't unrealistic—he knew being in love worked for some couples.

It wouldn't for him. No way would he end up like his mom, diving into that romantic connection and, after disaster struck, ending up a faded imprint of her former self.

Having Bea in his life as a friend, dating other women casually after this whole marriage thing ended, being satisfied with the people he had and the relationships he valued rather than the ones that could destroy him—that would be enough for him.

Anything else wasn't safe.

By this time next Saturday, they'd be connected in one more way.

But like the map, it would be just on paper.

Chapter Five

"Ta-da!" Emma flung open the door of the secluded cabin and waved at the interior with a flourish. "I saved you the best one, Bea. I figured it would be super romantic for you and Jason—" her eyes blinked wide and darted between Bea and Brody "—well, Brody now…" Cheeks flaring pink, she scurried inside.

Here we go. "Home sweet home," Bea murmured, taking Brody's hand and tugging him into the warm, cozy cabin.

Her insides softened to marshmallow fluff at the effort her sister had put in. There were the standard touches—the bottle of champagne on ice next to a plate of chocolate-dipped strawberries, rose petals scattered across the bed. But Bea had seen the cabins enough to know that Emma didn't treat every guest to twin vases of out-of-season merlot-petaled ranunculus. Nor was it customary to display photos of major moments in Halloran history, from their grandparents' wedding pictures to all the siblings at Bea's graduation. Below the frames' glimmering glass, a fire crackled in the hearth. Sumptuous blankets draped across the backs of the two armchairs.

"I thought you'd need a place to retreat after filming." Emma's gaze flicked to the king-size bed.

Oh, God, the bed. Of course, there was just the one. And no couch, either. Unless one of them was planning on crashing on the hardwood floor, they'd be within arm's reach of each other on that bed.

It's no big deal. We've shared a bed before.

A smaller one than this, in fact, a number of times. Her double bed the night he was helping her pack to come home from Costa Rica. A queen the weekend they flew to Vegas for a friend's bachelor party.

Why did it feel different?

Instead of unearthing a potentially dangerous answer, Bea chose to focus on the silly towel animal peering at them from the nightstand. "You made me an elephant." She couldn't help grinning at her sister's inside joke and turned to Brody to explain. "When we were younger, we never got to go on vacation—Mom and Dad were always too busy with the ranch—so Grammy and Gramps decided to take each of us on a holiday when we turned thirteen.

And because Emma and I were so close in age, they took us at the same time, to a Mexican resort. One day, a housekeeper made us an elephant for our bed, and I loved it so much, I refused to let anyone undo it for the rest of the trip. I begged to bring it home with me."

"And then you spent two months trying to learn how to make one yourself." Eyes twinkling, Brody kissed her forehead. "I remember."

Emma looked full to bursting. "Okay, that's seriously sweet you filed that away in your memory, Brody."

He smiled, a little sheepish.

"Who knew he was such a romantic, right?" Bea said.

Snagging her hand and snuggling her against him, back to front, he said, "Untapped depths."

His hard chest at her back warmed her through her sweater. Bea fought to keep her eyes from shuttering at the tempting heat.

"Not untapped to my sister." Emma snickered. "Sorry. Juvenile. Couldn't help it." She shook her head and waved at the nook past the bed, where the space left by the design of the bathroom provided a small corner for a kitchenette. "There's tea, coffee, some snacks and treats in the minifridge. I made sure to stock you up on the good chocolate. Unless you're trying to squeeze into your dress—then Brody can eat it. Or not, given he's Mr. Anti-Sugar…"

"It's all good, Emma." His eyes flashed with a

"leave me alone with my fiancée" sort of intensity, which was silly, because who cared if they had time alone? Unless he was trying to make it *appear* they wanted time alone.

God, he was better at this than she was.

Emma's eyebrows shot up in understanding. "Right. I'm out of here. I'll see you in the morning." She bared her teeth, a comically wide grin. "Dress day!"

"Yay, dress," Bea said weakly. *Crap. Dress.* They really needed to add that, as well as *final tux fitting*, to Brody's list. Were those on the filming schedule for tomorrow? She couldn't remember. Her hands went clammy.

The second her sister shut the door behind her with a wink, Bea relaxed against Brody's chest. She shouldn't. She knew that. Being smart meant stepping away, managing her nerves on her own. But his warmth and strength were irresistible, especially when he looped his arms around her in a tight embrace, both muscled arms crossed over her collarbones and hands gripping her shoulders. He lowered his head until their temples pressed together.

His deep breath sounded close to meditative.

She clung to his wrists with both hands. Her heart hammered. Could he feel it?

Another purposeful breath.

"Are you visualizing walking down the aisle like it's a race?" she teased. Once an athlete, always an athlete. Contemplating success was his norm, and she couldn't imagine this wedding would be any different.

An impossible-to-understand grumble filled her ear.

"I missed that."

"You're not a race, Beatrix."

Who knew what that meant?

She could feel his heart rate pick up, too, thrumming against her shoulder blades.

"What am I, then?"

It wasn't a question she liked to ask often. Too often, the answer was *scattered* or *flighty* or *frivolous*.

His arms tightened a little. With his head still pressed to hers, his breath warmed her ear. "You're exquisite."

"Seriously?"

"Very. You're not a race. You're something to savor."

Every ounce of breath left her. Being sweet like this wasn't his norm. She choked in a gulp of air. "You don't need to say that. No one's here to hear it."

"*You're* here to hear it."

One more squeeze, and he let go, backing away with a chuckle that would have qualified as self-conscious from anyone but Brody. But that wasn't in his emotional lexicon, so it had to be something else.

She turned to look at him.

His cheeks were ruddy, and he was ultrafocused on unpacking his duffel from the top of the long dresser into one of the drawers.

"Brody..."

"Mmm?" The drawer closed with a thunk.

"This is okay, right?" She bit her lip. "Sharing a room?"

"We're going to be sharing space once we're home. We'd better get accustomed to living together."

"Yeah, but there we'll have two beds."

He stared at the sole sleeping surface. "It's so big, we won't even touch each other."

But a couple of hours later, after they'd double-checked their to-do list for the next day, watched half of *Thor: Love and Thunder* on his tablet and tucked into bed, there somehow didn't seem to be enough room. She'd packed her full flannel pajama set, thank goodness, and had the pants tucked into her socks and the top buttoned to her throat. Brody wore flannel pants, too, but he'd forgone a T-shirt for some reason and his chest alone was taking up half the goddamn bed.

He was using said natural wonder of the world as a pillow for his e-reader. With his end-of-the-day rumpled hair and tortoiseshell reading frames, he was the thing "handsome glasses man" stock art was made of.

She growled internally, squeezed her eyes shut and tried to sink into the luxe mattress.

He tilted his head, brow lifted.

"What?" *Maybe* that came out testier than she likely had a right to be. He was just lying in bed, and she'd seen him shirtless a zillion times, so it was fair that he wouldn't have thought to throw on a tee.

It wasn't his fault she was noticing things she shouldn't be noticing. That a few kisses on the cheek and snuggles were hammering holes into the walls of her control faster than she could patch them up. They'd kept things platonic for so long. Surely, they could maintain that. Her boundaries and barricades couldn't be that weak.

"You made a weird noise," he finally replied.

Oh. Not an inside growl, then. "Sorry."

"All good." Reaching over with the hand not propping up his e-reader, he tangled his fingers in hers. Refocused on his book but tracing a soothing rhythm back and forth along her thumb as his story reabsorbed him.

She kept expecting him to let go.

She fell asleep, anchored to his hand, to reality, to a sense of comfort.

Brody was warm and surrounded by stacks of delicious cookies. Just Bea and him, sneaking snickerdoodles from the tray of misshapen seconds at the back of Sweets and Treats on Main Street. She was a teenager again, so was he, and they were both laughing about the batch he'd botched. And the cookies were knocking on the door? Wait, that didn't make sense. A loud rapping prodded his eardrums, trying to drag him from the warm baked-goods cocoon. He couldn't move, though. His limbs were heavy, and there was a weight on his chest...

And then there wasn't.

A shriek joined the knocking.

"Brody, we slept in!"

He opened his eyes, surfacing from the fog of his dream.

Bea sat next to him on the bed, back poker straight and cheeks crimson. She stared at his chest like fleas covered it.

He paused, confused for a second, until realization sank in. *Oh.* That weight had been her head. They'd been snuggling.

Maybe not a habit they should let stick—they couldn't risk cuddling turning into something else— but damn, he'd slept better last night than he had in a year.

After shooting his pecs one last dirty look, she bolted from the bed, still dressed head to toe in those soft, should-have-looked-ridiculous pajamas.

If she thought the full coverage sleep set would fool his lizard brain, she had another think coming. Head-to-toe flannel would have just been a challenge, had he been sharing a bed with a woman at all interested in being stripped down to nothing. A woman who *wasn't* his best friend. Two criteria that were beyond critical, and two criteria Bea would never meet.

Which—maybe she had a point with buttoning

up past her pretty collarbones. Best to block out any instinctual temptation.

Pfft. He could do that.

Had been pretty much his whole life.

Bea flung open the door and started apologizing profusely to whomever was standing on the other side.

The person was not impressed. Her voice was low but snapping.

Time to boogie. Brody darted to the shower. By the time he emerged from the bathroom, wrapped in a kitten-soft towel Luke and Emma must have spent a fortune on to stock in all the cabins and rooms, Bea was in her robe and standing on the other side of the door, foot tapping.

Her gaze, softening into something he'd never seen her direct at him before, drifted down to the towel. Her teeth snagged her lip.

Warmth rose up the back of his neck. Weird, because she'd looked at him a million times before. When he rowed, he wore spandex tight enough to appear painted on.

And he'd never seen heat in her eyes directed at him.

Until now.

"How late are we?" His question came out a little strangled.

Her pained expression pulled him out of his confusion. The only thing he needed to focus on at the moment was his part in filming for today, and making sure Bea felt supported while doing hers.

"We need to be there in fifteen minutes for hair and makeup. They're pushing filming back by thirty minutes."

"Okay. We can do that."

And they did. Fourteen and a half minutes later, they were walking into the loft suite in the lodge that the film crew was using for all the hair, makeup and wardrobe, as well as to store some of the equipment. Getting ready was a blur. Powder brushes tickling his nose and Rashida tsking about how the brown of his cardigan clashed with Bea's long red sweater and the stylist dousing him with hair product strong enough to withstand a hurricane.

"First up—" Rashida consulted her clipboard "—I need footage of the two of you going through Bea's wedding bible."

Bea blanched.

Rashida arched an eyebrow. "Is there something wrong with it? You said you had it finished."

"Uh..."

The makeup artist bopped Bea on the nose with the tip of a brush. "Honey, you're losing all your color and I'm going to have to redo your foundation if you don't perk up. I promise, Rashida doesn't bite."

"No, I have the wedding bible." The corners of her mouth were tight. "I followed the checklist."

What was wrong, then? He sent her a questioning look, but she glanced away.

Rashida primped her own curls in a mirror. "In that case, we're going to start at the prep table and film the two of you going through it. After that, we'll shoot you confirming with all the vendors, and the cake tasting."

Bea stood, and Brody took her hand, whispering, "Plans first. Then we'll worry about the vendors and the cake."

They headed out of the suite and for the top section of the spiral staircase.

"I know," she said, "but—"

"Look at you two lovebirds." A gruff, more than familiar voice floated up from the great hall.

"Grandpa," Brody called down, letting go of Bea's hand and picking up to a jog. "I'm sorry—I was going to come for coffee this morning, but we slept in accidentally."

Hank Emerson sported a plaid shirt and faded jeans, but the beauty of the room's opulent yet rustic design meant he didn't look out of place. His frown was, though. Brody's grandpa erred on the side of relaxed fisherman as opposed to grumpy old man. Especially since he officially retired last year. He homed in on Bea joining Brody at the bottom of the stairs as fast as he would have a flash of a trout in the depths of a river.

"Hey there, honey. I hear you and my grandson are up to some shenanigans."

Bea's eyes went wide. "Hank, I—"

"Falling in love isn't exactly shenanigans, Grandpa."

Hank snorted. "If you say so, son." He checked around the room, presumably to see if anyone was listening, which Brody appreciated. "Your cousin and Emma seem to be pulled in by whatever the two of you are trying to accomplish here, and I appreciate it's mighty complicated with all this Hollywood hullabaloo, but the sham is plain to me."

"Grandpa—"

Hank held up a hand. "I'm not saying you won't get there. Goodness knows you have a fine woman in Bea, something you've never managed to see."

"Oh, Hank…" Bea tutted.

"I see her just fine," Brody said, tracking Rashida and her assistant as they came down the stairs. Hopefully they weren't privy to this conversation.

"I won't say a word. You know that. But if you don't do right by Beatrix—"

"The whole point is to do right," Brody whispered. "And it's not a sham. We're getting married."

"Sure would have liked to hear about that from you instead of your stunned cousin." Hank didn't keep his voice down for that complaint.

Brody winced. No way would the two women almost to the bottom of the stairs have missed that.

"I'm sorry, Grandpa, I—"

"Hello there, Mr. Emerson," Rashida said, all smooth Southern manners. "I'm going to need to steal your grandson and granddaughter-in-law-to-be from you. No rest for the stars of the show, you know."

After a quick goodbye and a promise to join Hank

for dinner, Brody followed Rashida and Bea over to the table.

Rashida directed them into place, eyes narrowed. "The two of you had better get your family members on board with this being a happy event soon. I can't have the mother of the bride or the grandfather of the groom voicing opposition at the ceremony."

"They just need a little time," he promised.

Bea's concerned expression stole some of his confidence.

He mentally added *smooth ruffled feathers* to his to-do list. Of all the things they needed to accomplish, that one seemed the biggest challenge.

Chapter Six

Going over the wedding bible served many purposes. The show needed it as a required component, of course, but Bea figured it worked for her and Emma as businesswomen, too. It was a subtle way of working in the options available to wedding parties without being super obvious in advertising the lodge. It also made her look organized—a bonus for her own business. She wanted people coming to her for wedding flowers to know that she understood how floral arrangements fit into the overall plan, and that she had the planning chops to make their flower suite beyond what they imagined.

Of course, the flowers she'd picked out with Jason's mom didn't suit.

The whole wedding didn't suit. Being the luxe option, diamonds and pearls blanketed the designs, with subtle touches of holly and evergreen. Ugh, why had she let someone else assert her opinions so much?

Either she did what her heart told her to do and ended up not fitting in with her family, or she did what she thought people wanted her to do. That choice always led to going through life feeling like she had a rock digging into her instep.

She and Brody were elbow to elbow at the crafting table. The stone fireplace and Emma's carefully draped evergreen swags provided their backdrop.

"This is going to be beautiful." Brody traced a finger along one of the sketches Bea had done of the arrangements for the altar and the reception. He pushed up his reading glasses. "Wow, that's a lot of pearls."

"I know." She wrinkled her nose and sent an apologetic look at Rashida, who was in the frame on the other side of the table. "I'm rethinking those. Pearls are classic, and would suit the venue and so many brides, but I don't know if they're me, or if they really say Christmas as I—as Brody and I—celebrate it."

Caution glazed Rashida's face. When she switched from producer mode to host mode, everything about her was practiced, effortless. Bea felt like her opposite.

After a pause, Rashida tilted her head and put on a thoughtful expression. "It's common for brides and grooms to second-guess their plans. I'm sure you know that from your work."

Bea nodded. "Sometimes it's the floral equivalent of cold feet. Sometimes it's sticker shock. And sometimes it's from taking too many opinions into account when making the original decisions. One or both of the bridal couple realizes there's something about the decor or the ceremony that doesn't suit them."

"I'm sensing it's the latter," Rashida said.

"It is. And luckily, with doing some of the flowers myself, I have time to make sure they better reflect who we are."

"Cut!" Bracing her hands on the table, Rashida shook her head. "You're killing me, folks. Your wedding is supposed to be the over-the-top version."

Emma, who'd been standing by one of the polished log pillars wringing her hands, rushed over. "Isn't there luxury in simplicity? It's literally part of the lodge's mission statement."

"As much as I love the lodge, Em, my wedding isn't about your mission statement any more than it was about Jason's mother's love of pearls." Business plans were not Bea's go-to. The day Emma had sat her down and made her craft one for Posy—complete with corporate speak—had given her hives. She hadn't inherited her mom's analytical brain, not like Emma and Nora. Bea had never felt like she was on equal standing with her more accomplished sisters. Emma with her master's degree and Nora being a pillar at the family ranch—in comparison, Bea worried she came off as a child's rubber ball, bouncing irrationally.

There's more than one way to be a businessperson.

Brody's encouragement broke through her self-doubt. And it also didn't hurt to take Emma's advice from time to time, both about having a clearly identified purpose to drive her business, as well as her "luxury in simplicity" statement.

"I know the original plan was to play up glitz and glamour, but I think I'd rather show how we can use the natural world in a sumptuous way," she said.

She grabbed a pencil and started to erase parts of her existing sketches, adding in white berries in place of the pearls in the bouquets.

Please, please, please don't require me to have a wedding that's a reminder of Jason.

Sure, it wasn't a real ceremony, not in the sense of them making a lifetime commitment to each other. But everyone around them would think it was genuine.

And beyond that—it felt wrong to push forward with old plans.

"This is going to mean some more quick thinking," Rashida warned. "And stop sketching off camera. I want shots of you making the changes. But I also don't want it to appear someone shoved you into a decision you didn't want. We cannot have the audience clueing into you having a different groom. Let's play it off as a supply chain issue—the pearls and rhinestones didn't arrive."

"Sure," she replied, putting her pencil down, but unable to stop her brain from whirring into design mode. Eucalyptus over here, white anemones with dark centers to add some depth over there, if she could get them. Subtle, picking up on what was already in the lodge…

Brody nudged her with an elbow. "Rashida's asking us to act worried at first, and then to come up with a solution together, Sparks."

"Oh, sure." Her cheeks heated from being caught while spacing out. "If that's what you want."

"Yes, and then to get footage of you checking the menus and prepping for the cake tasting," Rashida said.

"Got it."

Pretending a supply chain issue had emerged was harder than she expected. After Bea stumbled over her words three times, necessitating new takes, Brody caught her arms and turned her to face him.

"Hey," he said. "I know this isn't what we planned. But you have an unending well of Bea magic inside you." Hands gentle on her upper arms, he dropped his forehead to hers. "You can overcome a canceled shipment with your eyes closed."

Cupping her face, he tilted her chin up. He stole a soft kiss.

"Damn it, you two, the camera wasn't rolling," Rashida said, clapping her hands once. "Again!"

After she called "Action," Brody repeated his line and the kiss.

But this time, he lingered. His lips on hers, soft yet demanding. A hand in her hair that would for sure necessitate a touch-up from the set stylist. The taste of coffee and cinnamon. She didn't know if it was the romantic decor of the lodge or the knowledge that her business and her sister's required her to make every kiss look better than the resolution of a rom-com. Whatever the cause, she couldn't ignore the result: Brody was in the running for best kiss of her life.

Nah. Couldn't be. Why would the universe do that to her, taunt her with an amazing possibility and then snatch it away? Because it wasn't going to become a regular habit.

Mmm, but it was delicious. She rose on her toes, pressing harder against his mouth, parting her lips a little. He took the invitation with a gentle sweep of his tongue.

Warmth pooled in her belly.

Uh-oh.

Stumbling back a step, she sent him a sheepish smile.

Fine, *dazed*. Kissing her best friend had left her with a swirling head and an ache in her core.

He winked at her, squeezed her hand and turned back to the designs on the table. "Let's redo this. Who needs pearls in a bouquet? The only pearl I need is you."

She nudged him with her elbow. "Corny, Emerson." Sweet, though.

And strangely enough, she kinda wanted him to mean it.

An hour later, she had the flowers redesigned,

combining Christmas and the wilderness setting in a riot of different greens, white and a touch of gold. Loose and easy instead of the original tight, crisp designs.

She bit her lip and glanced at Rashida. If she saw anything approaching criticism on the woman's face, she'd probably cry.

Only awe met her. "You're an artist. One of my favorite parts of a wedding is the romance of the flowers, and you've got that in spades here. I cannot wait to see you bring it to life."

Bea grinned, and Brody's arm tightened around her shoulders. "It's going to be interesting to add foraging in the forest to our to-do list, but what's a wedding without some last-minute changes?"

Brody choked on air.

Oh, crap. She smiled, hopefully covering up his reaction. "Is it time for the food yet? I've been dreaming of the mini-Yorkshire bites since we had them at the engagement party my sister threw for J—"

"Cut!"

Bea groaned. "I'm sorry."

Rashida sighed. "The rest of it was good. Say it again. Do it well, and I'll make sure you get extra cake during the tasting."

She followed instructions, mentioning the engagement party but not Jason, and then flipped to the food section of her planning bible. It wasn't possible to DIY the food early and keep it fresh, so the self-made component would be in the presentation of the dessert table, custom-making tiers and towers for a cupcake stand.

She pointed at one of the stands. "Let's trim it in velvet ribbon instead of the adhesive diamond strips. In fact, Emma has a stunning food display tiered thing already—wood and branches that mimic the staircase rails. Let's use that and add in some DIY components in some other way."

Something like a whimper came from Rashida.

Bea shot the woman a small smile and grabbed a page marker, flagging the stand for later.

"I'm more excited about the food itself," Brody said. To the untrained ear, he sounded genuine, but she caught something in his tone that was a little off. His finger went to the labels of the five cupcake flavors she and Jason had picked to sample.

Peanut butter. Pecan. Hazelnut.

Jason loved nuts, and Bea didn't have a preference, so he'd picked peanut butter filled with jelly, butter pecan and hazelnut chocolate.

And Brody had a nut allergy.

Not wanting to force the director to yell "cut" and waste everyone's time again, Bea nodded and schooled her features into a smile. She'd already seemed super indecisive more than once this morning. Any discussion about changing the menu would need to be subtle, so long as the camera was rolling. "I'm feeling good about the mint chocolate one and the pineapple one."

"Me, too." Brody pointed to the list of appetizers.

"Maybe we could get the chef to do the lamb popsicles in rosemary and mint instead of the soy-peanut glaze. Feels like it would match better with those Yorkshire bites." He glanced at the camera and smiled, as rich and delicious as the food he described. "It's all she's been talking about since the spring."

"I can't wait." To test the food, and to kiss his beautiful mouth again.

Bea startled at the thought. She wasn't supposed to want to kiss Brody. That went against every rule she'd ever made for herself in order to maintain their friendship code and keep him in her life.

Platonic. Affection, not intimacy. Keep any recognition of him being stinking hot in the objective column of her brain.

But this marriage exercise was erasing lines and chipping away at previously solid boundaries.

She was worrying about not wasting the crew's time and making sure the show and wedding turned out well—was that distracting her from a more important problem? If those boundaries crumbled, it could shake the foundation of their friendship. Even destroy it. And then what would they have?

Brody stood on the other side of the room, with the spiral staircase as his backdrop. The on-the-fly interviews were quickly becoming his least favorite segments to film. He was no stranger to interviews, on camera no less, as it had been a common part of competing internationally. But these daily inquisitions were a whole different animal. Even though *DIY I Do* was supposed to be heartwarming and positive, the director's questions felt pointed, like he was trying to get Brody to say something silly. Brody knew reality TV involved staged answers but hadn't expected to feel set up, not after how carefully Rashida had been monitoring Bea's various flubs all morning. Maybe Mark had a different take from the host.

"All right, Brody, you know how this goes." Mark appeared to be a decade or so older than Brody's thirty-two years. "I'm going to throw some questions at you, and you'll answer them. But you need to answer them as if you're just offering this up in conversation. If there's a part of the question the audience will need to know for your answer to make sense, you need to work it into the conversation."

He groaned internally. Not the "Will this be your last Olympics?" banter he was used to. Despite the unease churning in his belly, he nodded. Out of the corner of his eye, he could see Bea watching him. She didn't look that much happier than his stomach felt.

He sent her a quick smile before focusing on the camera.

Mark made a hand signal to the camera operator. "Your fiancée stumbled over some of your plans during the review session just now. Are the two of you having doubts, or is it just a case of indecision?"

Bea let out a squeak.

"I have never been surer of anything in my life than I am of marrying Bea." He didn't have to lie about that. Despite the stress of lying to their families, he was convinced this was the best way to go. Given he'd known early on he'd never get married, he'd never entertained the idea of having a wedding. But throwing a giant party for their family and friends, and having it themed to the things that mattered to Bea and him, was turning out to be kind of fun. So long as anything nut-related stayed far away from the kitchen. Thank God he'd caught that glitch.

"What about the two of you changing your minds on things?"

"Planning a wedding doesn't come quite as naturally to me. If it doesn't involve knitting needles, I'm hopeless in the DIY realm. Seeing it coming to life rather than on paper made it obvious where we need to put more thought into it."

"But you've had over six months to prepare," Mark said.

"Six days, six months—doesn't make me more or less crafty. But the most important part of this week, other than saying 'I do' at the end, is making sure it's the day of Bea's dreams. *Our* dreams. Though, given mine is essentially to make her happy, I'm good to follow her lead."

The director nodded, as if convinced. "Bit of a contradiction to your competition years. I did some research on your rowing career. You were the stroke seat. Didn't that make you the leader?"

Brody grinned. "There are parts of being in a relationship that's like rowing crew—working together, being in tune with each other, finding balance. But when it comes to a wedding, I'm happy to sit in a middle seat."

"The middle?"

"The engine. The effort. Take direction, follow the stroke seat's lead. Important, but doesn't set the pace. And Bea is an excellent leader."

He caught her wide-eyed expression on the edge of his vision. Damn, he wished she felt more confident. Yeah, she'd had a few missteps during the first filming segment, but wasn't that expected? They weren't exactly on-screen professionals.

"Are we done here?" Brody asked Mark. "I was promised cupcakes."

Mark frowned, as if unhappy he didn't unearth anything salacious, but nodded and pointed to the table by the window where the lodge's pastry chef was setting up her offerings. "Head over there next."

To the table of death.

He hurried over, hoping to catch the chef before Mark called for action. She introduced herself as Maelle and shook his hand. She had light brown skin, a thick, dark braid and a vaguely European accent. Maybe she was from Switzerland or something. Being a ski town, Sutter Creek got people from all over the world, and the baked goods she'd laid out would suit a high-end resort in the Alps.

Her mouth twisted. "You look like a man who's about to tell me you don't like buttercream."

"No." He kept his tone low. "I look like a man who's about to tell you that I have a moderate nut allergy. I need to know which products I can and can't eat, but without it seeming obvious on camera."

Brown eyebrows knit into a dark slash. "The notes said the groom *wanted* nuts. I made the cupcakes exactly as specified."

"Right. Thing is... I'm not the original groom."

The chef's double take was epic.

"I know. Not the usual practice. And not something that's going to make it into the TV episode. But that's neither here nor there. Can we get through the tasting strategically, without me breaking into hives?"

Rashida came over. "What's the problem?"

"I have a nut allergy," he said.

"Are you kidding me? It won't be much of a cake tasting if the groom can't try any of them."

"I know. Nor would we want to waste all the effort Maelle has put in here." Or cut down on displaying the full range of what the lodge kitchen could do. "I'll just eat what I can."

"The vanilla-base flavor should be okay," Maelle broke in. "But I can never guarantee—"

"As long as the tools weren't used for two flavors at once—"

"Never." The chef looked like it was akin to kicking puppies.

"I figured not. I'll stick to the nut-free ones, and it should be fine."

Rashida crossed her arms. "Are you sure? The last thing we need is for you to have a rash and fish lips. Or worse, a visit to the emergency room due to anaphylaxis."

He shook his head. "I regularly eat in restaurants without issue. It's been years since I had a reaction. Bea can eat all the nut ones, and no one will be the wiser. Let's show off these cupcakes for your viewers."

Chapter Seven

Bea was approaching glycemic coma levels. Zero regrets.

"Maelle, you are a freaking sugar-and-butter goddess. Oh, my God," she mumbled around another bite of the hazelnut chocolate that Brody was subtly avoiding. He'd cut into it with a fork and moved some of the icing and crumbs around to make it look like he'd taken a bite.

She pointed to one of the other options with her own fork. "I think that one's the winner, though. The mint chocolate is a perfect replica of Brody's grandma's brownie recipe. Lighter, of course, but the exact flavors. She made them year-round but only added mint at Christmas."

A corner of his mouth lifted. "You're right. I thought it tasted familiar but couldn't place it. Embarrassing." He glanced toward the ceiling. "Sorry, Grandma."

Maelle's smile, which had been stiff since Brody's allergy reveal, softened. "By the looks of all your grandmother's notes, she loved being in the kitchen. I'm tickled you recognized my homage."

Bea nodded. "When my sisters and I were small, we would come over with our own grandmother and would bake in Mrs. Emerson's big kitchen." Realizing they hadn't explained much of their family connection for the camera yet, she added, "Brody's grandparents used to own the lodge, and the property borders my family's cattle ranch. Our grandmothers were best friends."

"And I reaped the baking benefits." He patted his stomach.

It had been a rare day he hadn't walked out of his grandma's kitchen with a brownie in each hand. And usually, Bea had been on his heels, toting a pair of her own.

Though she was almost sugared out, they had one more flavor to taste. She plucked one of the pineapple-filled confections off the tower of samples.

"The mint chocolate was all about Brody's family's Christmas traditions, but this one's mine." She had to hand it to Jason; he had remembered that pineapple was her favorite dessert flavor. For all his flaws, he hadn't been entirely unobservant. "It's not related to the holidays, but it's been my favorite since I was a kid. I'll be honest. One of the main reasons I competed so hard for that theme park job was to have daily access to the frozen pineapple whip. Let's see if this is similar."

Brody snatched one, too, and scooped a glob of icing onto his finger. He held it in front of her mouth with a twinkle in his eye.

Well, if he insisted... She closed her lips around his fingertip. Her eyes shuttered as the creamy texture melted on her tongue. Acid and fruit, not too sweet, like sunshine in the tropics. The pad of Brody's finger was velvet against her tongue, too. Odd, because she knew his long hours coaching on the water and the rowing machine roughened his skin, but in her mouth...

Oh, jeez, she was sucking her best friend's finger on tape. She jerked back.

"That's...yummy," she squeaked. "Reminds me of snacking while watching fireworks in front of the castle."

Brody bit off half of the cupcake in one chomp, then put the rest on his plate and licked his fingers. "You are not kidding. That's delicious."

"I think we'll go with those two options," she said. "And is there a way to do the butter pecan, but with butterscotch instead of pecan? That one was so good, too." There was that time she visited a friend in Denver, and they'd found an epic donut shop where the desserts had droppers of whiskey in them... "Oh!"

She quickly pulled up the picture she'd taken of her donut. "Could you do something like this? Vanilla cake, buttery icing and actual scotch in a dropper? Grown-up butterscotch?"

Maelle blinked. "Uh, if I can get the droppers…"

Bea nudged Brody. "We could use your favorite scotch."

"Sure." His forehead creased, and he ran his tongue along his lips a few times, then his thumb.

She flashed to seeing him do that in a restaurant once. A buffet in Vegas for that bachelor party they'd gone to together, when a mislabeled dish included pine nuts, not sesame paste.

She grabbed his knee. "You're having a reaction."

"A bit, yeah," he admitted, looking sheepish in his discomfort.

"You need Benadryl." She kept her voice low. "Or maybe your EpiPen."

He shook his head. "It's not that bad."

"Cut!" Mark said.

"You didn't eat the nut ones, did you?" Rashida asked.

"Of course not."

Maelle paled. "There shouldn't have been contamination."

Brody's eyes closed, and he scratched his reddening throat. "It wasn't you, Maelle. It was my fault. I fed Bea off my finger, and then I ate with that hand."

An uproar hit the set. Concern mainly, though Bea heard Kaitlin muttering to someone else, wondering about how the hell that error was possible. A crew member trained in first aid swooped in to attend to Brody, shuttling Bea aside.

She circled behind his chair and put a hand on his shoulder. "Should we go to the hospital?"

"Maybe. It's not bad so far," he said.

Fear prickled her neck. "You're the one having the reaction, but if my vote counts, I think we should. Just in case."

"Your vote counts, Bea." He took her hand.

She wanted to lift their joined hands and kiss the back of his, but jeez, that could make things even worse. Brody's allergy was usually at the front of her mind when they were out to eat or she had him over for dinner. She was *not* used to the rules around kissing.

"I shouldn't have pushed with this." She swore under her breath. "We should have just tasted the ones that were safe—"

"I was the one who stuck my finger in your mouth, Sparks." He sighed. "But yeah, my mouth and throat are itchy."

"You should use your EpiPen," she said. "Before it gets worse."

The medic seconded Bea's suggestion.

"It's mild," Brody grumbled.

"It might not be in a minute or two," she said.

Brody raised his eyebrows, making it clear he thought she was overreacting, but pulled his EpiPen out of the back pocket of his jeans and followed the steps to use it. "This stuff makes me feel like garbage."

"So does anaphylaxis," she said, her mild tone belying the guilt roiling in her belly, threatening to build into panic. "We need to get you to a doctor."

Rashida nodded and pinned Bea with a look. "Call me the minute you find out what's happening."

Mark and Kaitlin sidled up to Rashida. "If Brody can't film later today, we should shift the dress fitting to this evening."

More like *dress making*, but Bea figured now wasn't the time to bring that up.

Rashida shot a dirty look at her director and assistant. "Let's decide that later, okay?"

"I still don't get how this happened," Kaitlin said, ignoring Bea and Brody. "He saw her eating nut cupcakes! And wouldn't she know not to eat something off his finger?"

Ah, being talked about when you were standing *right there*—always great.

Bea didn't want to think about the dress and how much work it needed—she needed to focus on her miserable fiancé.

"We made a mistake," she told the PA. "It happens, especially since none of this is exactly normal for us. And right now, I'm not worried about my dress. I'm worried about Brody and making sure his throat doesn't close over."

"Of course," Rashida said.

Kaitlin mumbled an apology.

"This isn't that serious a reaction," Brody groused.

"It's common practice to transport via ambulance," the medic reminded them.

"*No*," Brody insisted. "The car is fine."

Bea turned to him. "Let's get to it, then. And don't even think of driving. Do you have a backup EpiPen in case you need it?"

"Yeah, on top of the dresser in the cabin."

"I'll run and grab that. Someone needs to take you out to the car. I'll meet you there." Bea waited for his nod before addressing Rashida and her assistant. "I'll call once we know what's going on. I wouldn't count on us being back anytime soon. The last time I went to the hospital with Brody because of a reaction, it took hours."

"I'm sorry." His hand was starting to shake in hers. A sign the medication was working, but she knew from watching him go through this before that it wasn't pleasant.

"We'll make do." Rashida didn't look thrilled about the idea, but more concern than annoyance filled her gaze.

"Thanks." *Make do*. Really, it was the motto of the week. Hopefully, Brody wouldn't end up super sick because of it.

Five hours later, Brody trudged down the path to their cabin, Bea on his heels. She'd been his shadow at the hospital. It was now around eight. The property dark and private but for the lights lining the paths and the porch lights on the row of cabins. No sign of the film crew, who was no doubt off somewhere panicking about the schedule change.

Bea unlocked the door to their cabin and waved him inside.

"You can stop fussing now." Brody aimed for a reassuring smile.

The room was warm and cozy, the fire crackling behind the glass shield of the hearth. "I take it Luke or Emma popped in here when you texted them to say we were on our way back?"

Bea nodded. She was still paler than normal. While waiting for his symptoms to subside, she'd babbled on about feeling responsible. Unnecessary. It was an oversight, one mostly of his making, and he'd been the one to pay the price.

Well, the production had, too. He and Bea would no doubt have to make up for the lost hours. She'd been covertly texting with Rashida while they were in the ER. He hadn't had the energy to ask for updates. His reaction hadn't affected his throat or his breathing, but the nausea and stomach pain had wiped him out, leaving him foggy and shaky.

He gripped a chair while he toed out of his shoes, feeling too wobbly for comfort. Reaching for his jacket zipper with shaking hands, he turned sideways from Bea so she wouldn't see him struggle.

"Hey, silly goose." Her voice was feather gentle, a soft swipe of care across his abraded composure. She came around to face him, swatting his hands away.

Careful fingers unzipped his jacket, slid it from his shoulders and tossed it on the chair, and then went to work on his button-up shirt. "No need to be a hero. I can help."

In another world, it might have been a turn-on, having a beautiful woman undress him. But not a woman he'd sworn not to think of in those terms, and definitely not in a post-ephedrine haze.

But then she went for his T-shirt, too, and his heart skipped a beat. "What's your endgame here?"

Her cheeks reddened, and she snatched her hands back, leaving the cotton layer in place. "Getting you ready for bed." She pointed at the bed. "Sit."

He perched on the edge of the plush mattress, too tired and queasy to care about grasping a modicum of independence.

She thrust his pajama pants at him. "Put these on. Do you need anything else to eat?"

Shaking his head, he slipped out of his jeans and into the soft flannel. He yawned.

"Brush your teeth, then, and I'll tuck you in."

"Bossy," he teased as he headed for the bathroom.

Once he'd dealt with his teeth, he came back out. The turned-down covers on his side of the bed welcomed him. Bea sat cross-legged on her side, watching him with guarded concern.

"I'll be okay, Sparks." He let the mattress take his weight and then let Bea slide the heavy comforter over him.

His assurance didn't erase her frown. She was a

bit of a mess, her sunshine curls tousled in six different directions and her camera-ready makeup faded. God, she was precious, though. The only person in the world he'd want to have at his side during long hours at a hospital.

Lip sandwiched between her teeth, she paused for a second before snuggling against him with her head on his pillow and her arm over his chest. Warm, vanilla-scented breath teased his neck. Even though any visible inflammation had gone away thanks to sweet, sweet antihistamines, he'd have thought any stimulation would irritate the still-sensitive patches of skin. It didn't. The soft breaths, matched with the calm rise and fall of her chest against his arm, soothed him.

He unearthed his arms from the covers so that he could hold her properly. Yeah, he was the one who'd been sick and he sensed her need to smother him with care, but his urge to make sure she was coming down from her own panic lurked below the surface.

"We don't need to snuggle," he said. "We're not on camera."

"I know." She burrowed closer.

"You don't need to feel guilty, either. I was the responsible one."

"I should have been aware, too," she said. "You heard everyone wondering about why we both would have made that mistake."

"Easy to do."

Her nose scrunched. She buried her face against his shoulder.

He bent the arm he'd looped around her and rubbed the base of her skull with his thumb and finger. The short curls at her nape twisted around his finger and thumb, the strands silk against his skin. It made him wonder, just for a second, what other parts of her would be like satin, smooth and touchable. That fraction of a thought couldn't harm anything. It wasn't long enough to be of significance, to disrupt their safe balance.

She grumbled something he didn't catch.

"I missed that," he rasped.

"Rashida needs me back over at the lodge."

He almost sighed in relief. Her leaving would be so much safer than her lying here, every inch of her soft and comforting against his side.

"You sure it can't wait? It's getting late." *Oh, Christ, Emerson, let her go. Don't turn this into something it's not.*

"No. I need to get my dress done."

Right. She'd been working on her dress for months, stealing hours of time whenever Jason worked late. "It's not bad luck that I've seen you work on it?"

She lifted her head and cocked an eyebrow. "I don't think there's such thing as bad luck when the marriage isn't going to last."

"I guess. And I have to admit, it'll be fun to see you walk down the aisle wearing something you made."

Her lips parted.

Only the threat of another allergic reaction stopped him from leaning forward and stealing a kiss from that surprised mouth.

Which… *What the hell?* This was *Bea.*

Bea plus kissing—when a camera wasn't involved, anyway—wasn't an equation with a positive solution.

"I don't want to leave," she said.

"The doctor cleared me. I'm not going to have another flare-up."

Her arm tightened over his chest. Another hint of vanilla, maybe from the cupcakes, teased his nose. She wasn't a vanilla person, not by any measure, but the warmth and inherent sweetness of the scent suited her. Matched the way she'd always been his safe space. His home, really.

"I'll be okay alone," he said.

Will you, though?

For crying out loud. Nothing like a few hours in a hospital to get him to a place where he was asking himself questions he'd always refused to answer, even with the battery of mental health experts he'd worked with during his time as an athlete. They'd accepted his "I have lots of friends and supportive family; I can't give enough to a romantic relationship right now" explanation.

So why wasn't his heart buying what he was selling anymore?

"That scared me today," she said quietly. "And it sucked to be partly responsible."

"I'm okay. You should go do what needs to be done. All that beading…"

"I know." She sighed. "But this is nice."

"It is." His voice was way too rough. "Seriously, go do your thing."

And maybe by the time she got back, he'd have gotten his head on straight.

Chapter Eight

Bea wrapped her cardigan around herself and bustled across the night-kissed property to one of the lodge's staff entrances, into the hallway that separated the kitchen from the great hall. The thin knit, colored a festive green and spangled with gold, wasn't half as effective at warming her as Brody's embrace had been.

Unsurprising. The man had suspense-movie-hero arms and always put off a ton of body heat. He'd warmed her up with a hug many a time.

The look on his face, though, an unfamiliar mix of contentment and revelation and alarm—*that* wasn't anything she was used to.

She had to shelve her curiosity. Not only was it

dangerous to contemplate how snuggling with her had put Brody in a space where he was having revelations, but she needed to stay sharp for the dressmaking session. She hustled through the doors into the great hall and over to the nook off the dining area where she planned to work on her gown. The small crew was set up. Just a couple of tech people and Mark, Rashida and Kaitlin huddled together. Rashida stood, loose-limbed and expression unfazed—a contrast to the stiff shoulders of her director and assistant.

Bea smiled, hating how it wavered. "This nook is one of my favorite places on the property. When Brody and I were younger, we had some epic cribbage battles on the old coffee table." Said coffee table was, of course, gone, along with the rest of the dilapidated furniture. Emma had replaced the dated decor with sleek pistachio-green velvet couches and side tables with slate tops. Someone had shoved the new coffee table to the side to make room for Bea's dress.

It took every ounce of her to suppress a groan.

Hanging on a sewing form, the silk shone. Light caught on the beading. In all the places where there *was* beading, anyway. The complete bodice glittered, tiny seed pearls and crystals sewn in tiny flowers like her grandmother had taught her to do as a child. The hem, though… Not even close to finished. Four months of working on it when she could, and the gaps were still obvious.

Damn it. The wedding dress was supposed to be

one of the crowning DIY components, tied into her family and her business through the skill and the motif.

Her stomach roiled. Had she oversold?

Hours and hours of sitting, beading alone while the camera rolled and Rashida or Mark asked her questions, would be tedious at best and uncomfortable at worst.

"This probably won't make for riveting filming," she said. "Me, alone with a needle and thread?"

"You won't be alone." Her sister barreled into the small space. Emma, patting Bea's arm to punctuate her pronouncement, wore an A-line candy cane-print dress that made her look like a holiday pinup. Nora followed, in her usual jeans but sporting a gold sweater that definitely counted as dressed up by her older sister's definition. The garment was probably Emma's, and Bea's heart squished that Nora had put in the effort to borrow something thematic.

A lump rose in Bea's throat. "You came."

"It's your *wedding*, Bumble," Emma said. Bea was so touched they'd come she didn't even make a face at her sister using that infernal nickname. Emma gave her a squeeze. "We're your bridesmaids. And we pricked our fingers learning to bead flowers with Grammy just as much as you did. We're in this to the end."

"Is Mom coming?" she said, forcing the words past the lump, almost managing to sound calm and not desperate.

Taking a seat in the armchair on the left side of the dress, Nora winced. "Mom pulled early ranch duty. She's going to take a pass on this round."

A logical excuse.

Entirely unbelievable, too, given the way Nora focused on the hem of the dress instead of meeting Bea's gaze.

"How about me? Will I do?" A deep voice came from behind the camera operator.

"Jack?" She spun. It was only Sunday, so her cousin's crooked grin and hands-in-pockets sheepishness threw her for a loop. "What happened to arriving on Thursday? Since when are you ever early for a family event?"

"Your wedding isn't any old family event." Jack's rumpled dark hair suggested he'd just gotten off the plane from his Oregon home. His T-shirt hung a little off his muscular frame. He was still too thin after having spent the previous winter and spring smoke jumping in Australia, followed by a long summer and fall battling various blazes from British Columbia down to California.

She launched herself into his arms. He was here, and he was alive—neither ever a guarantee, given his line of work—and joy burst in her chest at getting to hug him, despite the shadows haunting his eyes. She'd ask him about those once the camera was out of their faces. Jack had always understood her better than her sisters or younger brother, finding her wanderlust and big dreams exciting rather than a source of derision. When her parents had taken over raising Jack and he'd moved permanently to the RG Ranch as a rebellious preteen, he'd gotten her into trouble every second day, and she'd loved each minute of it. Each minute of seeing him find his place and heal from his grief, too.

Helping cheer him up had probably helped her know what to do when Brody lost his dad, come to think of it.

Oh, crap. He didn't know about Brody.

She glanced at the camera and then backed away from her cousin.

He was still grinning. "You and Brody."

Ah, he had heard, then. She tried to match the confidence of his smile.

"Meant to be," he continued. "Always thought so." He held out a hand. "Give me a needle. Looks like you've got work to do."

She blinked at him. "You want to help us with beading?"

"Ah, she forgets I mend my own parachutes and make my own jumpsuits." He lifted his gaze to the ceiling and sighed exaggeratedly. "If you all focus on the sparkles, I'll get those seams cleaned up and I'll fix the fit in the back."

She put a hand to her chest. "What's wrong with the fit in the back?"

"Nothing, once I'm done with it." He winked. "We're here for you, Bea. All of us."

Well, not her mom. But for now, she'd take her

sisters and cousin, especially if it meant a finished dress before the sun rose the next morning.

"Oof, my fingers are going to fall off." Nora shook out her hand, no doubt to reestablish feeling in her fingertips.

Bea did the same. After six hours of sewing by hand, her own circulation was shot. She soaked in the rare feeling of peace between her and her siblings. When was the last time they'd stayed up until three in the morning together?

"The cramps are worth it. We have a dress." Emma's green eyes glowed brightly in the portable lights. "And it's gorgeous."

Jack, who was sitting next to Bea on the couch, looking smug after having fixed all of Bea's off-kilter darts in the lining, nudged her with a shoulder. "Dress of your dreams, cuz?"

She stared at her creation—*their* creation. Her eyes wanted to take it all in at once. Impossible, given the beading spanned yards and yards of fabric, but she tried to soak in the whole. "I think it is. We did it."

"Try it on," Emma insisted, then scooted off in the direction of the kitchen.

"No," Rashida broke in. "That's scheduled for to-morrow afternoon."

"This afternoon?" Yawning, Nora stood and stretched.

The host nodded. "Yes, that would be more accurate. We need all hands on deck for it, too, so y'all need to go get some sleep." She glanced at Bea. "And you and I need to be back here at eight for flower arranging."

Emma reappeared with a platter of cupcakes. "First, we snack. We deserve it."

Jack had one in each hand and Nora was licking frosting before Bea could even squeak in protest.

Emma sent her a knowing look. "They're not the nut ones. You can go back and kiss Brody to your heart's content. But eat. I heard your stomach growling not long ago."

She capitulated, downing one of each of the pineapple whip and mint chocolate confections before sneaking back to the cabin.

A cozy-looking lump lay under the covers, right in the middle of the bed.

Though exhaustion weighed her limbs down enough that she'd be able to sleep on eight inches of mattress, let alone a couple of feet.

After brushing her teeth and removing her makeup, she shucked off her jeans and sweater and sat on the edge of the bed in her underwear and camisole. Maybe she'd just lie down briefly, worry about finding her pajamas in a second.

The next thing she knew, light glowed red through her closed eyelids.

Crud, had she turned on the bedside light and not realized it? She was under the covers. Warm, even.

She cracked an eye open. Not the lamp, but morning. And it wasn't the covers keeping her warm.

It was Brody.

Hair-roughened legs tangled in hers. A heavy hand splayed across her belly, strong fingers feathering her opposite hip bone. A hard, hot chest pressed into her back. And against her bottom—well, then.

It didn't mean anything. Just the usual morning situation for a guy.

But if it *did*...

It doesn't. That was for another woman to enjoy.

"Brody?" she whispered.

"Oh, hey." His palm drew a small circle on her stomach, his pinkie dangerously close to the waistband of her underwear. He then snatched it away, grabbing the half-full glass of water off her nightstand and downing it. Tucking his arm back under the covers, he settled his hand back where he'd had it. Palm now chilly, just for a second until it warmed on her too-hot skin. "What time did you get in, sweetheart? I didn't realize you were here until just now."

"Since when am I 'sweetheart'?"

"You're going to be my wife. 'Sweetheart' is a pretty small liberty."

Lord, his voice was something in the morning. Smoke and honey, a languid swirl, holding her in place just as much as his hand.

Wife. Her pulse skipped. "I didn't think we'd be taking any liberties."

Her own tone wasn't far off his rasp.

"A year's a long time, Sparks. Maybe we could allow ourselves a few." His lips teased the back of her head.

Wait just a second. This was not the Brody she'd gone to bed with. She turned to face him. "You don't do relationships. Not ones that stick."

"I know." His face twisted, disgruntled. "I'm not suggesting that."

"Be clear."

"We seem to be good at getting close," he said. "And it doesn't feel wrong."

She stroked a hand along his stubbled cheek. "Not sure that's the same as being right."

"I'm pretty sure it's whatever word we decide to use."

Her thumb was so close to his full lips. She traced the tip along soft, water-damp skin. "Right now, the only word I can think of is *temptation*. And that's weird for me, Brody. I've never let myself be tempted by you."

"Same." Gentle fingers brushed a few wild curls off her forehead.

Oh, jeez, she had to look a mess, not having taken her makeup off and with her usual morning bedhead. Her hair usually took on a life of its own the minute her head hit a pillow.

He didn't seem to care, though. He raked her with a wondrous gaze, the deep brown only getting richer as he leaned forward.

His breath teased her lips, then his kiss.

The softness of it, the gentle heat, kindling something inside that seemed utterly strange yet perfect. His mouth was cold from the water he'd tossed back.

She jerked away. "I haven't brushed my teeth in hours."

"You taste like chocolate cupcakes." He sounded amused.

"I didn't eat any more nut ones."

"I trust you." His fingers threaded through the hair at the back of her head, pulling her toward him with the barest amount of pressure.

Because, good Lord, she was willing. Despite everything going on, everything about who they were and their friendship, kissing him had become vital to her existence. Why else would her heart be thrumming loud enough to echo in her ears? His touch was a gust of oxygen on the embers low in her belly. His hands, one on her nape, one low on her back, could ignite her like a match. Bossy fingers spanned her lower spine, teasing the strip of skin between her underwear and camisole. He held her hips to his length, insistent, barely leashed.

Maybe that *wasn't* just morning wood. Maybe he actually wanted this.

And that—that wasn't something to rush into, not with Brody.

Breaths jagged, she put a hand to his chest. "We need to think."

He stared at her, slack-jawed and chest rising and falling like he'd finished a sprint. "Right. Thinking."

"Maybe when we're not in bed, in our jammies." If she could even call her panties and camisole *jammies*.

"Good point," he murmured, plucking one of her

thin shoulder straps with a finger. "Along with you all of a sudden being a temptation, you're also a damn fine distraction."

Fighting the magnetism of his hard body, she scooted back a few inches. "I'm not used to this."

"Yeah, it's new."

And, as always, something new gave her a thrill. The hungry maw within, forever demanding a steady diet of excitement, lapped up the possibilities of discovering something wonderful. But marrying Brody for the sake of her business and the lodge, for the sake of her pride, was entirely different from actually being with him. He wasn't a shiny new thing. Their relationship gave her more of a foundation than any other in her life. She couldn't risk losing that, not for the sake of a few kisses.

"This is a bad idea." She untangled from him, body protesting the loss of warmth and goodness. Being close to him was far too easy.

He reached for her, snagging one of her shaking hands. "Not sure you're right on that."

She tugged her fingers from his grasp. "I can't be impulsive about this, Brody. About you."

"So put some thought into it, then. And talk to me. Tell me what you're feeling."

She shot him a rueful smile. "If I knew, I would."

The river burbled, running cold and crisp around Brody's knees. He was nice and dry from the waders that covered him from his chest to his toes, but

the chill still seeped through the waterproof material. He cast his line with the methodical flicks and
sweeps his grandpa taught him decades ago.

Said mentor stood ten yards downriver, casting
with the skill of a master.

"River has a way of clearing your mind, doesn't
it, son?"

"Usually," he said. Not today, though. He doubted
his jumble of thoughts would even untangle were he
to duck his head under the frigid water.

That kiss he'd shared with Bea, the fact they'd
admitted to temptation and the floor hadn't caved
in around them—he didn't know what to make of
any of it.

"What on God's green earth made you think this
was smart?"

Had Hank read his mind? His cheeks warmed.
"Well, we are sharing a cabin..."

Hank waved him off. "Not that. That's your business. I meant the marriage. Marriage is a sacred in-
stitution. Not something to make a mockery of."

He sighed. "The show can provide publicity for
Bea's shop and the lodge."

"That's not what I meant, either. I've watched *DIY
I Do*. Reality TV will never make much sense to me,
but I do see the host and the show being respectful
of relationships and ceremonies."

Brody flicked his fly as close to the nearest riffle
as possible. He didn't care much if there was a fish

under the rippling water. He needed the meditation of it, not the result. "What *did* you mean?"

"That marrying someone in jest is dishonorable."

Brody's footing wobbled. His grandpa's disapproval wiped him out like one of the periodic log jams that flowed down the river. With his mom being emotionally inaccessible for most of his teen years and beyond, he'd relied on Hank—and his grandma, until her death—to be his touchstone.

"It's not in jest. It's not typical, I agree. But it's not a joke to me. I have a chance to help Bea with something important—something important to our family, too—and I can't step away from that."

Hank's fly sailed over the water. "You love her, then."

"Of course I do." He'd never let himself be *in* love with someone, but he loved her. "As much as I'm able to, anyway."

His grandpa's gaze softened. "Never doubt love, Brody. It's what knits a soul together. Knits two souls together, if you let it."

Exactly what he couldn't do. When you knit part of yourself to another person, it made you unravel when they were torn away.

He checked his watch. "Shoot, I need to get back up to the lodge to help Bea with flowers."

Hank paused midcast, the line fizzling onto the water way off target. "Flowers? You?"

"I think the producers want to get some shots of me looking foolish. But Bea's good enough that it might cover up my ineptitude." He grinned. "Thanks for the chat. And don't worry, I'm not going to do Bea wrong."

It took him a few minutes to get back up the trail to the lodge. Damn it, he was going to be late. He needed a shortcut. The tackle room, from which he'd borrowed his chest waders and fishing gear, was on the other side of the basement. He could cut through the shiny new casual café, change and then hop up the spiral staircase to the great hall and hopefully not be too behind schedule. The Alert: Live Filming sign on the door had been up there for days, so he assumed it was a generic warning.

He blew through the basement doors in a gust of November wind. Voices greeted him. Passing the glass-backed indoor waterfall, he stopped short.

The transformed café area filled in as a dressing room of sorts, with the usual couches arranged into a big semicircle around a circular carpeted pedestal. A temporary curtain was set up in front of one of the walls. Emma and Nora were in their bridesmaids' dresses, sweeps of gold-sequined fabric. Nora stood barefoot in front of one of the couches, while Jack Halloran, pins sticking out of his mouth, worked her dress hem with precise stitches. Two cameras were catching the action.

"Jeez, Nor, have you ever worn a sequin in your life?" Brody asked, approaching the group.

Nora shot him a dirty look.

Emma flicked her hand in his direction in clear panic. "Brody! You can't be here! Bea's about to—"

The curtain parted and Bea floated through. Brody caught a glimpse of cream fabric and glitter before Emma launched herself at him and covered his eyes.

"You can't *see her*."

"It's okay, Em," Bea chided.

"No, it's not!"

"I've already seen it," he reminded everyone. "She's been working on it for months."

"But that's when it wasn't for—" Emma cut herself off with a hiss, no doubt remembering the cameras were capturing her every word.

Delicate fingers pried away the makeshift blindfold.

"Hey," Bea said, voice edging on nervous.

He blinked, getting his focus back. It was impossible to take in all of her at once. Too much to look at: the delicate silk fabric, beaded flowers sprinkled across the bodice, swirling around her waist in an asymmetrical swath, spilling down the skirt in a cascade of tiny crystals and pearls.

"I—" He reached out a hand, but damn, he had gloves on and no way could he touch her, all gritted up after fishing. Devouring her with his gaze instead, he soaked her in.

It wasn't enough. The urge rose to pull her close and taste her mouth, coax those teeth to release their hold on her lip.

"What do you think?" she asked.

"I guess I need to wait to kiss you in the dress until the big day."

A mischievous gleam lit her eyes. "Yes."

Her clasped hands strained, as if she was trying not to wring them.

He peeled off one of his gloves, plucked her hands up with his newly bare one and kissed her knuckles. "You look… You're always gorgeous to me. But this is something else." He'd let himself recognize the many ways she was beautiful. Her joy, her verve. Always in flashes. Always in parts.

Not as a whole. She'd be his wife—temporary, but still fully his—this unbelievable combination of big personality and generous love, and yeah, she was a knockout, too.

The fabric of her dress skimmed her curves like it was made for her.

It *was* made for her.

Am I made for her, too?

He laughed. *Not likely.*

"What?"

"Just blown away by you. And that you're going to be my wife." For long enough that their families wouldn't ask questions, anyway.

"Your wife," she said, sounding a little breathless.

He chanced a glance at Emma, who had the same look on her face she got when she watched Christmas rom-coms with his grandfather. Cocking a brow at his soon-to-be sister-in-law—that, in and of itself, was a trip—he motioned to his fishing getup.

"I should change. Promise I'll clean up for the ceremony."

Bea's smile twitched. "You look fantastic in anything."

"Or nothing?" he murmured. He couldn't help it. Yeah, he and Bea knew that wasn't on the table, but everyone else would expect that kind of teasing. Damn, they needed to get some time alone, create new ground rules given they were violating their old ones six ways to Sunday.

"Cut!"

Cheeks pink, Bea swatted his arm. "You can't wreck the footage like that. No innuendo."

Rashida sent him an exasperated look. "At least you gave us some solid romance before you took it to a place my show does not go."

"Sorry," he said.

But given it had earned him that blush from Bea, he wasn't sure he meant it.

Chapter Nine

Brody tapped his foot and twisted another wire, careful to make a perfect loop of the beads he'd threaded in a glittering row. He fumbled with a bead, earning a fond smirk from Bea. He shrugged, returning her smile. It was like every painful afternoon he'd ever spent trying to learn how to tie flies with his grandpa, never being as good at it as Luke.

His amateurish skills didn't matter, though. He was happy to help with whatever work Bea needed completed. She was a few feet away, up to her ears in freshly harvested evergreen sprigs, some flat green stems, puffy white flowers and some flatter, wider-petaled ones that he'd thought were poppies, but she'd called anemones.

"What are these loops for again?" he asked, laying another next to his growing row.

"They'll add some glitter to the bridesmaids' bouquets." Squinting at the monstrous arrangement in front of her, she moved one of the ball-shaped flowers. "Mine, too. Similar to the faux diamonds and pearls of my original design but coordinating with my dress."

"That's me, bringing the bling." He chuckled, unable to keep a straight face.

She snorted. "Oh, always."

"You know me. Gold's always been my favorite color."

"So says the wall of medals in your town house."

His stomach dropped. "It's your house, too."

Her hands stilled. The stem she was holding snapped audibly. "Uh, right." She glanced at Rashida. "We were waiting until after the wedding to live together. I'm, uh, in the process of moving my things over from my old place."

Mark waved a hand. "It's okay. We can edit that part out. Keep going."

Brody gritted his teeth. How many shots of this did they need? They'd been arranging flowers for what felt like a decade. Bea's quick fingers and skilled eye, him fumbling and helping where he could. Were they never going to get a minute to themselves? He'd have thought that in the week leading up to a wedding, the bride and groom would get at least a few moments alone. But alone didn't seem to exist when they were busy with twelve-hour days of filming.

Tomorrow wouldn't be any better. They'd be tromping all over Sutter Creek, getting hometown footage. And after that, Bea would be finishing the decorating on Wednesday and Thursday… At least she'd solidified her vision for something rustic, elegant and a little wild.

Was she happy with it?

It was impossible to talk about anything of substance while the cameras were rolling. And Christ, they needed to have a serious conversation. Putting down his pliers, he stole another glance at her. A disgruntled wrinkle marred her forehead.

"What's the matter, Sparks?"

"Something's missing." She fiddled with the riot of greenery crowding the table in front of them.

Nudging her with an elbow, Brody winked at her. "I don't see how, given it's the size of a small elephant."

She poked him in the biceps. "The lodge fireplace defines 'soaring.' Anything less than substantial will look off balance."

"I'm teasing. It's gorgeous."

"It is." Her hands landed on her hips. "But is it Christmassy enough?"

"Let me look at it from your angle." He circled behind her and looped his arms around her shoulders, crossing his forearms over her collarbones and bringing her against his chest.

The inside of his wrist brushed the smooth skin exposed by the wide neck of her sweater. The innocent touch was a pinball setting off a cascade of lights and bells in his body.

Her breath caught.

Maybe she'd felt the zing of desire, too. He wanted to ask, but couldn't, and it ate at him. How were they supposed to focus on flowers when they had more important things to hash out?

She sagged against him. "The old design wasn't what I wanted, but the pearls did add a certain something."

"Does it need more koala food?"

That earned him an elbow in the gut. "The eucalyptus is perfect."

"I agree." The whole creation was perfect, in his opinion, but he wasn't the professional, and his business wasn't on the line. He could keep her relaxed, though. "There's no way to hang tinsel on it and call it a day? I always lived to throw tinsel on the lodge trees."

Except for the rare holidays his dad had been stateside, his mom had never managed to gather up enough emotional energy to have a tree at the house. His grandma had made sure to include him in the lodge's decorating traditions. Every year of their childhood, he and Luke had strewn gaudy silver handfuls all over the trees his grandpa cut fresh for the entryway and the great hall. He'd stopped asking to be included after his dad died, but the decorating tradition had continued. Emma had done an impressive job with the current great room showpiece, which centered the two-story windows with the pomp of an opera diva. White, gold, silver and enough ribbon to swathe the castle of the theme park where Bea used to make preschoolers' dreams a reality.

"Tinsel?" She tilted her head and cocked an eyebrow. "I'm assuming you're kidding."

"Of course." He kissed her temple. "But is there a way to pull in something that one of us has always done with our families?"

Covering his crossed forearms with her hands, she dipped her lips to kiss his wrist.

A soft, innocent press.

For now.

Earlier, it hadn't been. She'd kissed him like she wanted more.

So did I. Then, and now. What would it be like if those lips of hers drifted elsewhere? Along his mouth, his neck...

Okay, that needed to stop, like, yesterday. Her curvy ass pressed right against his twitching dick. If he couldn't muster some freaking self-control, she'd figure out exactly where his thoughts had drifted. Not to mention the intrusive lens of the camera.

They needed to talk, and not to have the entire StreamFlix audience privy to their business. All this wedding stuff was stopping them from figuring out what their life was going to look like once they married. Would they delve into some sort of physical relationship? And what would that look like? Friends with benefits wouldn't cut it. They were too close for that.

"Tradition-wise, I was thinking we should set up your family's German Christmas pyramid," she said.

He blinked, trying to shift from sex back to the reception. "Uh, I thought we were decorating with flowers and the swags Emma already put up."

"We are. But the pyramid's important, too. A reminder of your grandma, and so pretty with the candles and the Twelve Days of Christmas carvings."

He nodded. "Grandma had all her glass ornaments, too, but I don't suppose those would work in a bouquet."

"No, too clunky." She sighed. "I'm going to think about it."

"With five days until the wedding?" Rashida cut in.

Bea sent the producer a confident smile and then craned her neck to look at Brody with mischief in her eyes. "Sometimes the best things happen when there's a time crunch."

Rashida moved to be in frame. "All right, you two, it's time for a bit of a surprise. Every *DIY I Do* wedding has a homemade feature from someone other than the bride and groom." She motioned to the doorway.

Luke, Hank and Bea's dad, Rich, came through, each carrying an armful of birch logs. They were all wearing collared flannel or cotton shirts tucked into crisp jeans, a notch dressier than usual.

"Dad? Are we setting up the fireplace?" she asked, snagging Brody's hand and then stepping toward their family members.

Rich's booming laugh filled the great room. "Not hardly, sweetheart. We spent days on these things. We've been waiting to give them to you and…you and Brody for weeks."

The three men stacked the logs on the table. Each one was hollowed out.

"Are they vases?" Her hands flew to her mouth.

"I found a dead birch when I started to string lights for the holiday light stroll," Luke said. "Grandpa figured we could buck it up and put it to use."

"How did you get this idea?" Shock bled into her tone.

"Emma's had me on Pinterest, coming up with ideas for the lodge since we created our partnership," Hank explained. "I thought you'd love this."

She snatched the largest one and plunked it next to her creation. One swift motion and she transferred the arrangement. "It's exactly right! It hints at Christmas without hammering anyone over the head with red and green."

Edging on sheepish, Hank rubbed the back of his neck. "Happy to help. Nothing but the best for my new granddaughter."

"Or for my busy Bea." Her dad circled behind the table to give her a hug. The look he shot Brody carried more than a hint of warning.

Bea's eyes glinted with tears as she glanced between her dad, Hank and Luke. "Thank you."

"Cut!"

Finally. Brody's shoulder muscles eased, dropping by a good inch. Wrapping Bea's shaking form in a hug, he glanced at Rashida. "Did you get what you needed? Are we done for the night?"

She drew back. "Are you having a problem with the hours?"

Just that they're stopping me from being alone with this woman.

"Honestly? Today? Yes. We've barely had a second to ourselves. I miss time alone with my fiancée."

"It's okay," Bea jumped in, sniffling. She pierced him with a shut-the-hell-up look. "We get it. It's part of the deal. Sorry about the crying. I'm just touched by the gesture of the vases."

Part of the deal. Right. This wasn't about the tangle of need and confusion in his chest. It was about making her look good. Thankfully, his terse words hadn't been caught on film.

"I'm sorry," he said, meaning it.

"Thank you," Rashida said. "And, Bea, you'll never hear me complaining about tears. *DIY I Do* might aim for a lack of manufactured drama, but I still want gobs of emotion. Viewers lap it up."

Tightening his arms, he bent his head to his sniffling fiancée's ear. "They might love it, but I don't like seeing you cry."

"These are good tears," she said.

Rashida's smile softened. "All this is normal. Emotions are always high the week before a wedding, and the filming exacerbates them. But we are done for the night. Go. Take a breather. Have some alone time."

Alone time, with Bea. He wanted that. Craved it. But was it what they really needed?

Bea followed Brody into the cabin, her stomach unsettled by his touchy mood.

Swinging the door shut, she reeled on him. "What's been up with you today? Joking one minute, cranky the next… Are you okay?"

He slung his lean body into one of the armchairs and unbuttoned the second button at the neck of his shirt. He jammed both hands into his hair. "I'm sorry. I know, I need to keep my priorities straight. Today was hard, though. Flipping from one thing to another, the roller coaster of seeing you in the dress and then making the flowers with you and then having our family show up. It's…it's real, Bea. In some ways."

Keeping her eyes off that tempting V of skin he'd exposed at his collarbone, she toed out of her shoes and padded over to the chair next to him. The side table between the two arms, graced by a lamp, divided them like a mountain range. But crawling into her best friend's lap, giving in to the urge to be close, was such a big no.

Or was it? She couldn't ignore the heat she'd spotted in his gaze over the course of the day. And then there was the flame flickering deep in her core, demanding his hands make it burn even stronger…

She swallowed. "It does feel more real than I expected."

"The wedding?"

"Yes. And—"

Should she admit the temptation rising to the surface? The scorching lava bubbling between the cracks of her self-control? Brody hadn't changed. He didn't want a commitment, and this was still a temporary arrangement.

"*And,*" he echoed. Not as a prompt. His tone didn't suggest he expected her to finish. The knowing emphasis spurred her to bravery.

"Are we going to see other people while we're married? Quietly, of course?" The words tasted like garbage on her tongue. But really, a year of staying celibate seemed a lot to ask of him.

The handsome angles of his face shifted in revulsion. "Cheat on you? Are you kidding me?"

She lifted a shoulder, forcing nonchalance. "We haven't talked about it yet, and it'll be a while until we can convincingly split, and—"

"I'm *not* going to be unfaithful. Never."

"But—"

Elbows on his knees, he fixed her with a sincerity that touched all the way to her marrow. "I can't do forever. But I can sure as hell keep my fly zipped for a year while I'm *married* to you."

Relief washed through her veins. "I wasn't sure."

"Be it on the water or the altar, when I decide to do something, I do it. I'm going to marry the hell out of you, Beatrix Halloran."

She almost chuckled. He was decisive—that had never been his problem.

So why won't he decide to love someone?

Not for her sake. But for his. Yeah, people could live perfectly full lives without a partner. After this debacle ended, she might end up being one of them. She brought her heels to the edge of the chair and hugged her knees to her chest. She knew why he wouldn't reach for forever. Everything he'd seen with his mom, losing his dad—love scared Brody. He wasn't living partner-free because it made him happy. He was doing it because the alternative might hurt him. And because of that, she needed to guard against letting her affection for him and this ridiculous, newfound urge to jump his bones grow into something romantic. She'd kept things separate for so long, though. She knew how to compartmentalize with him.

"Not sure it will be easy," she said softly.

"Bea, I came back from injuries and disastrous races to win gold, which I did in large part because I knew your smiling face was in the stands, cheering me on. Being roommates is a piece of cake compared to rehab and coming back after losing at the Olympics. Delicious cake. Like, six layers of that butterscotch buttercream you asked the pastry chef to make."

FREE BOOKS GIVEAWAY

2 FREE ROMANCE BOOKS!

2 FREE WHOLESOME ROMANCE BOOKS!

GET UP TO FOUR FREE BOOKS & TWO FREE GIFTS WORTH OVER $20!

We pay for everything!

See Details Inside

YOU pick your books –
WE pay for everything.
You get up to FOUR New Books and TWO Mystery Gifts...absolutely FREE!

Dear Reader,

I am writing to announce the launch of a huge **FREE BOOKS GIVEAWAY**... and to let you know that YOU are entitled to choose up to FOUR fantastic books that WE pay for.

Try **Harlequin® Special Edition** books featuring comfort and strength in the support of loved ones and enjoying the journey no matter what life throws your way.

Try **Harlequin® Heartwarming™ Larger-Print** books featuring uplifting stories where the bonds of friendship, family and community unite.

Or TRY BOTH!

In return, we ask just one favor: Would you please participate in our brief Reader Survey? We'd love to hear from you.

This FREE BOOKS GIVEAWAY means that your introductory shipment is completely free, <u>even the shipping</u>! If you decide to continue, you can look forward to curated monthl shipments of brand-new books from your selected series, always at a discount off the cover price! <u>Plus you can cance any time</u>. Who could pass up a deal like that?

Sincerely

Pam Powers

Pam Powers
For Harlequin Reader Servic

Complete the survey below and return it today to receive up to 4 FREE BOOKS and FREE GIFTS guaranteed!

▼ DETACH AND MAIL CARD TODAY! ▼

© 2022 HARLEQUIN ENTERPRISES ULC
and ™ are trademarks owned and used by the trademark owner and/or its licensee. Printed in the U.S.A.

FREE BOOKS GIVEAWAY
Reader Survey

1
Do you prefer stories with happy endings?

◯ **YES**   ◯ **NO**

2
Do you share your favorite books with friends?

◯ **YES**   ◯ **NO**

3
Do you often choose to read instead of watching TV?

◯ **YES**   ◯ **NO**

YES! Please send me my Free Rewards, consisting of **2 Free Books from each series I select** and **Free Mystery Gifts**. I understand that I am under no obligation to buy anything, no purchase necessary see terms and conditions for details.

❑ **Harlequin® Special Edition** (235/335 HDL GRM5)
❑ **Harlequin® Heartwarming™ Larger-Print** (161/361 HDL GRM5)
❑ **Try Both** (235/335 & 161/361 HDL GRNH)

FIRST NAME   LAST NAME

ADDRESS

APT.#   CITY

STATE/PROV.   ZIP/POSTAL CODE

EMAIL ❑ Please check this box if you would like to receive newsletters and promotional emails from Harlequin Enterprises ULC and its affiliates. You can unsubscribe anytime.

Your Privacy – Your information is being collected by Harlequin Enterprises ULC, operating as Harlequin Reader Service. For a complete summary of the information we collect, how we use this information and to whom it is disclosed, please visit our privacy notice located at https://corporate.harlequin.com/privacy-notice. From time to time we may also exchange your personal information with reputable third parties. If you wish to opt out of this sharing of your personal information, please visit www.readerservice.com/consumerschoice or call 1-800-873-8635. **Notice to California Residents** – Under California law, you have specific rights to control and access your data. For more information on these rights and how to exercise them, visit https://corporate.harlequin.com/california-privacy.

SE/HW-122-FBG22_SE/HW-122-FBGVR

◈ HARLEQUIN® Reader Service — Terms and Conditions:

Accepting your 2 free books and 2 free gifts (gifts valued at approximately $10.00 retail) places you under no obligation to buy anything. You may keep the books and gifts and return the shipping statement marked "cancel." If you do not cancel, approximately one month later we'll send you more books from the series you have chosen, and bill you at our low, subscribers-only discount price. Harlequin® Special Edition books consist of 6 books per month and cost $5.24 each in the U.S. or $5.99 each in Canada, a savings of at least 13% off the cover price. Harlequin® Heartwarming™ Larger-Print books consist of 4 books per month and cost just $5.99 each in the U.S. or $6.49 each in Canada, a savings of at least 20% off the cover price. It's quite a bargain! Shipping and handling is just 50¢ per book in the U.S. and $1.25 per book in Canada.* You may return any shipment at our expense and cancel at any time by calling the number below — or you may continue to receive monthly shipments at our low, subscribers-only discount price plus shipping and handling. *Terms and prices subject to change without notice. Prices do not include sales taxes which will be charged (if applicable) based on your state or country of residence. Canadian residents will be charged applicable taxes. Offer not valid in Quebec. Books received may not be as shown. All orders subject to approval. Credit or debit balances in a customer's account(s) may be offset by any other outstanding balance owed by or to the customer. Please allow 3 to 4 weeks for delivery. Offer available while quantities last. Your Privacy — Your information is being collected by Harlequin Enterprises ULC, operating as Harlequin Reader Service. For a complete summary of the information we collect, how we use this information and to whom it is disclosed, please visit our privacy notice located at https://corporate.harlequin.com/privacy-notice. From time to time we may also exchange your personal information with reputable third parties. If you wish to opt out of this sharing of your personal information, please visit www.readerservice.com/consumerschoice or call 1-800-873-8635. **Notice to California Residents** – Under California law, you have specific rights to control and access your data. For more information on these rights and how to exercise them, visit https://corporate.harlequin.com/california-privacy.

BUSINESS REPLY MAIL

FIRST-CLASS MAIL   PERMIT NO. 717   BUFFALO, NY

POSTAGE WILL BE PAID BY ADDRESSEE

HARLEQUIN READER SERVICE
PO BOX 1341
BUFFALO NY 14240-8571

NO POSTAGE
NECESSARY
IF MAILED
IN THE
UNITED STATES

▲ If offer card is missing write to: Harlequin Reader Service, P.O. Box 1341, Buffalo, NY 14240-8531 or visit www.ReaderService.com ▲

"But I…"

He was all rangy power, loose limbs and testosterone.

Her mouth went dry.

His eyebrow lifted. "But you…"

"Something about getting engaged, and thinking about being with you for a year, and sharing a bed…" And the kissing. Oh, God, the kissing. "I mean, I've never been attracted to you before. Or let myself be, anyway."

She'd expected him to break in with a teasing "jeez, thanks" or a feigned wound to the ego, but he stilled.

He didn't say anything at all, just waited with his brown gaze tender.

"I am now, though. Attracted to you. And as long as we're roommates, I'm not sure it'll go away. Even though we won't be sharing a bed." She let out a sigh, worn out by the admission.

He nodded slowly. "It's part of what set me off-kilter today. I wanted—want—you. And I know I shouldn't."

She wasn't sure if knowing he felt the same way made it easier or harder.

Or if it means it's inevitable that things will go somewhere unexpected.

"We're the ones making the boundaries, though. We can decide what does and doesn't work for us," she said. "No point in torturing ourselves by insisting on being celibate all year. And if neither of us are comfortable seeing other people, then all we're left with is—" she wiggled a finger between them "—us."

Her heart thrummed. Ugh, why was he just sitting there staring at her, not saying anything? Somehow managing to look as delicious as a tray of macarons but also like the object of her frustrations.

He ran a hand down his face. "We have something good, Bea. I don't know if we should risk it."

But what if we find something more?

She cringed at the unwanted thought. That was the whole problem: Brody would never do more. Emotionally, anyway.

Restlessness crawled along her limbs. Emptiness. A whisper in the back of her mind that this man could take her to places she'd never seen, never felt. His kiss had promised endless pleasure.

And that, she wanted. Even if the emotional half would be forever out of range.

Rising from her chair, she scooted in front of him and sat on his plush footstool.

He fixed her with a questioning look. "Remember that conversation we once had?" Whatever memory was on his mind pulled his mouth into an amused curve. "About what it would take for us to make out?"

Ah. *That* memory. She chuckled. "How many drinks we'd have to have before we kissed, you mean?" Yeah, she remembered. It was foggy, because they'd been rather drunk at the time they'd joked about it. In a bar outside London, celebrating one of Brody's crew's many victories, when he had half the women there hanging off him. It had been light-hearted, their estimation of a pitcher of beer apiece.

They'd never tested the theory.

"And here it didn't take an ounce of alcohol." She leaned forward and pressed a kiss to his mouth. Threading her fingers in his hair, she persisted until he groaned, parting his mouth. "It took a ring."

"So traditional," he mumbled midkiss.

She laughed.

He joined her, until they were both out of breath and tears were streaming down her cheeks and he had his arms around her.

Was it the funniest joke? No. But getting to laugh about the absurdity of the situation opened a pressure valve, releasing tension that had been building to catastrophic failure levels for days.

He stared at her in wonder, eyes lit as if she was vital to his happiness. Brushing her tears off her cheeks with his thumbs, he kissed her. Consuming. Any hesitation, any doubts vanished after their shared crescendo of laughter.

"Sparks," he said, the endearment pitching into reverence. "Anyone ever tell you you're a damn good kisser?"

"No, actually." The admission threatened to dim the joy of being in Brody's arms, consumed by his hot mouth. Her taste in romantic partners left a lot to be desired. Even now, with the best man she knew, she didn't have something that could last.

But that was okay. She was used to fleeting experiences, brief bursts of joy and excitement that she savored in the moment and then let go once it was time to move on. She'd do the same with Brody—delve into the closeness of him, explore the pleasure they could bring each other, and then when it was time to move on, to return to only friendship, they'd do that.

Soft lips trailed along the side of her neck. She ached to feel them elsewhere. All over her body.

"You're irresistible," he said, words gritty as if he were fighting them. "I could taste you for days."

Her cheeks heated. "I'm okay with that."

Serious brown eyes met hers. "I guess we have more than a few days for this. A year's worth of them."

"Yeah. And then we move on. Back to being friends," she said. "We would know it began and ended in bed."

The silent query turned to disbelief. "Sex complicates things between friends."

She laughed. "We're getting *married*. What's more complicated than that?"

He shook his head.

"What?" she said.

"I was about to say *not for real*, but it is for real."

"Yeah."

"Even if we're not in love." The truth scorched her like underage whiskey, rough, leaving a burn.

"Right," she murmured.

His hesitation should have made her want to pull back, to return to her seat, to go to bed with a figurative—or maybe real—pile of pillows stacked in the middle.

It didn't.

Nothing sounded better than leaning forward and plucking the rest of Brody's shirt buttons open, one by one.

She'd stopped herself from seeing him as eligible for decades. Surely she could stop herself from falling in love with him for a year. "I don't want to fall in love with *anyone* right now. Not after misjudging Jason so badly. I need time to trust my instincts again."

"And what are your instincts saying right now?" He tugged at his collar and flattened his hand, skimming it over the placket of his shirt to rest on his flat belly.

"To climb on your lap and have my way with you."

His throat bobbed and his voice was a croak at best. "Bea. Sweetheart."

"Okay." Embarrassment burned up her neck. "It's a no, then. I get it."

And she was going to hide the rest of the night, because damn, it was a thousand percent crappy to get turned down. Shooting to her feet, she strode toward the safety of the bathroom. "I'm going to soak in the tub," she called over her shoulder.

Forever.

The chair creaked and heavy footsteps followed her. Hands landed on her hips and pulled her back from the doorway. "No, you're not."

Her pulse jumped. *Yes.* "Says who?"

Demanding hands tugged her flush against his front. One wide palm caressed her stomach. The other pressed over the notch of her collarbone. His teeth grazed her earlobe. "Me."

"What made you change your mind?" Her voice was barely a whisper. What if she didn't like the answer?

"You." His own whisper kissed her temple. "No woman compels me more than you, Beatrix Halloran. So as much as every alarm bell I've ever programmed to sound is ringing in my head, I cannot keep my hands off you."

"Oh," she breathed. *Oh.*

Good, *good* answer.

A breath later and he spun her to the bed, laying her out, bracing over her on an elbow and a knee.

"Can't keep my mouth off you, either." His lips claimed hers for a hint of a second, a blink, before trailing along her jaw and settling in the base of her neck. Teeth scraped on her collarbone. Every inch of her lit up, and she arched toward him, seeking the heat of his body, the rock-solid planes of his hips and thighs.

She planned to soak up every moment she got to figure out what made Brody tick, to revel in the feel of him against her.

Who had time for tentative? Screw that. She was diving in. Her palms soaked in his warmth, the smooth skin of his back, the dusting of rough hair on his pecs, the angles of muscle and bone. All things she'd seen before but cataloging them with her fingers was a whole new joy.

A possessive hand pushed her hip to the bed and held it there as he nuzzled and laved, slowly making his way along the low V of her sweater.

She squirmed against the weight of his hand.

"Stay still, Sparks." The weight shifted, a quick skim up her belly, taking her sweater with it and over her head.

"You're dreaming," she said, hooking a leg around the back of his thighs. Somehow, some way, she'd find the antidote to the yearning building at her core, and it sure as hell wouldn't involve being motionless.

"You're a dream, all right," he mumbled against the valley of her breasts. A thumb traced the edge of her sheer bra. Teased its way across the whisper-thin fabric to one of her nipples. He groaned, mouth following the path he'd forged. "God, you taste good."

She clutched his hair, holding him there, where his tongue danced a quick rhythm around the peaking nub. Her head swam and her blood sizzled. Brody was enjoying her body, which went against every expectation she'd ever set in her life. And she could get drunk on that alone, on the power of hearing him moan. But more than that, he knew how to flick his tongue just right. A chain of sensation linked her nipple and her core, and finally, *finally* there was enough pressure between her legs to erase the emptiness.

Uh, his hand, you mean?

Brody's fingers drew a hot path over her leggings. She'd been so lost in him sucking and teasing her nipples. Adding in more stimulation, so close to her center, sent her spinning. She stiffened, gripping his shoulders.

He stilled. "Too much?"

"Wasn't expecting it."

"Sorry." He withdrew his hand. "I assumed that's where you wanted me to go. Should have asked."

She stared into his eyes, deep brown and all-consuming. "Since when do I not love the unexpected? It's perfect, Brody. This is perfect."

"I have an even better idea."

He shifted down the mattress, not wasting any time in sliding off her leggings. His breath seeped through the fabric of her underwear, singeing her self-control. The flash of triumph in his eyes, the sexy tilt to his mouth, aroused her even more. His confidence skated across her intimate flesh as he made an unspoken promise he knew exactly how to make her fall apart.

Insistent lips pressed against cotton. A thumb on her center. Tension coiled the demand for more, for nothing between his soft kiss and her building need. Rough fingertips teased the hollows between her thighs and her mound. Her hips lifted, pushing back against his leisurely nibbles.

"Strip me," she said, ready for the physical vulnerability, ready for whatever it took to get his mouth on her naked skin.

"Gladly." Hooking a finger under the delicate band of fabric, he worked her panties down. A low hum of desire—of appreciation—escaped him, kissing her sensitive bud.

Another languid lick, a gentle kiss.

She sifted a hand through his hair. "So tentative."

"No, unhurried." He spread her thighs with his palms and nuzzled, licked. "Gotta do this right, Sparks."

Her nickname was so very accurate at this moment. Points of heat, of light, shimmers on her skin and building between her legs.

Every breath, every flick of his tongue and feast of his lips, she slipped under his spell.

"Wait." She had to push the word past a cry of want. "We should come together."

"We've got plenty of time for that," he promised, sliding a finger into her wetness. "Tonight, I want you to fall apart while I kiss you."

She whimpered. She craved sharing pleasure with him, but it was so easy to give in to his insistence, the skill of his teasing strokes and building kisses. Heat cascaded along her belly, her thighs, every bit of skin that he worshipped and stroked.

Another finger, another hint of fireworks and flashes.

"But—"

"I love this," he said, voice low and rasping. "Finding the secret parts of you, tasting you. Knowing we want each other, and we can explore that. But it's about you right now." He curved his fingers inside her, pressing, finding the spot that made her vision blur.

"Yes, Brody, there..."

"Mmm, yes. Tonight's about you. Just you."

His words, the pressure pulled her under. Into the bright light and blitz of weightlessness.

Into euphoria.

And when he slid back up the bed and stripped to his boxers, pulled the covers over them and held her, she let herself relax into his strength.

Her hand drifted along the planes of his chest, arrowing toward his own pleasure. A palm pressed her hand against hard muscle, trapping it in place. "Let's snuggle for a second."

"You don't want to come, too?"

His lips curved against her forehead, no doubt a teasing smile. "We have a year. There's no need to race."

She rose on an elbow and walked her fingers back up his chest. God, she wanted to make him forget his name, forget where he was, forget everything except how good it felt to have her mouth coaxing him toward oblivion. "But you live for races."

His laugh was rough, like his attempts to stay in control were costing him. "I live to win, Bea. And I already won here."

She shot him a disgruntled look. "It's not a win if it's one-sided."

"Relax. It's early yet."

"Hmph." She nestled in, enveloped by his warmth and strength and the tattered end of her pleasure. This *was* nice.

More than. Enough to buffet her against the onslaught of the week. Exhaustion crept in around the gilded edges of the best orgasm she'd had in years. It weighed her limbs, and she sank farther into Brody.

His arms tightened and he kissed her hair. "There you go."

"I'm not forgetting about you, I promise."

"I know. Five minutes of this, and then we'll worry about me."

"Fine. Consider the clock started." They did have time. This wasn't forever, and it wasn't love, but it was good.

Chapter Ten

Brody stole one more kiss from Bea as she locked up their cabin, earning a scolding squeak.

"Sorry," he said, not meaning it one iota. "Didn't mean to distract you."

"Yes, you did."

It was near impossible to leave their cozy, private nest this morning. After the night they'd spent together, bringing her pleasure he'd never allowed himself to contemplate, all he wanted to do was take her back to bed and make her moan his name again.

The keys jingled in her hand. "I'm going to drop them if you don't stop."

"They won't break."

She shot him a dirty look. "I can't believe you let me fall asleep on you last night."

Not the first time she'd scolded him since waking up. "You needed it."

"No, I needed to know that things were reciprocal."

"Hey." He nipped the petal-soft skin below her earlobe. A particularly sensitive part of her body, or so it had seemed last night when she'd nearly levitated off the bed at the slightest flick of his tongue.

She let out a ragged breath.

He smiled against her skin, falling under the spell of the delicate, barely there floral scent of the moisturizer she'd applied this morning. Her hands had slicked over her body, tempting him to be the one to take over, but she'd been too busy reaming him out for not waking her. He'd missed the chance to insist he get to help. "We can worry about me another time."

He'd live. Or at least he could survive a few hours, having taken care of himself in the shower this morning.

Fine, the middle of the night, too. She might have passed out like she hadn't slept in a month, but he'd lain there awake for hours. Holding her, reliving the sounds of her ecstasy and her salty sweet taste on his tongue. He'd eventually sneaked out of bed for a brief respite from her tempting, naked body. He sure as hell wasn't going to spend much time thinking about why it had felt like the most natural thing in the world to kiss Bea until she cried out in abandon. Or how the second she offered to do the same, it felt like too much. Like something he'd been craving his whole life but that also sent him into cold sweats. It didn't make sense how it could be both.

She harrumphed and finally managed to lock the door.

A throat cleared at the bottom of the stairs. "Sorry to interrupt, but..."

"Oh!" The keys landed on the wooden porch. Bea grabbed them and whirled to face Kaitlin. "You startled me."

Protectiveness, overbearing and entirely unnecessary, washed through Brody.

"Again, sorry." Kaitlin didn't sound at all sorry, but at least she didn't have a camera operator with her. It was way too early to be filmed. She sighed. "You two are just that cute, aren't you?"

That was the point. They were getting good at pretending. Though it didn't feel much like pretending this morning. Not now that he'd had the taste of her on his tongue.

"What can we do for you?" he asked. "Shuttle's in fifteen, right?" They were all up extra early to film at the bakery in town before the breakfast rush arrived.

A curt nod. "I wanted to get you the call sheet, in case there's anything you need to bring with you. It's short notice, I know, but Rashida had extra work to do with securing filming locations and permits. *I* had extra work to do. It's a busy day." She shoved a folder at them. "Rashida had me call and ask your parents for ornaments for you. She's figured out a logical reason for why you'd be decorating a tree here."

"What?" Bea's jaw dropped. "I thought we'd agreed *not* to decorate a tree."

Kaitlin lifted a shoulder. "Take it up with Rashida." She spun around and strode toward the lodge.

"What the hell?" he whispered. Damn it. He couldn't avoid the quick flash of his dad's smile as he lifted Brody, eight years old and full of innocence, to fix the star to the top of the tree. His stomach sank, then twisted, shaken like a still-closed pop can.

"I don't know." She opened the folder and held it for them both to see.

The schedule listed the day's filming locations.

Sweets and Treats Bakery—breakfast.
Sutter Creek Canoe and Kayak Club dock—
Brody rowing.
RG Ranch—trail ride.
Halloran house— tree decorating.

He jabbed the paper with a finger. "How does it make sense to decorate at your parents' place?"

Bea's gaze jerked to his. "It doesn't."

He didn't need to explain to Bea that he had mixed feelings about the activity and didn't want to share much about his family on camera. "Did you say something to Rashida at some point that would make her change plans?"

"Of course not." Her hurt tone made him wince. She shuffled out of his grip and crossed her arms over her winter coat. "I thought she didn't want us to decorate because it wouldn't be authentic. And I never would have suggested it. Not with your memories."

"I can't believe they called my mom." He jammed a hand into his hair. "She shouldn't have to deal with that. I need to see if she's okay."

"Maybe we could bring some ornaments from elsewhere so that she doesn't have to get involved." She chewed her lip. "But ideally, I want to get Rashida to cancel the idea entirely."

"Okay, let's divide and conquer, then. You find Rashida, figure out where her head's at. I'll go ask my cousin if he can round up some of the family ornaments for me. I agree I don't want to do it if we can avoid it. But if we have to, I don't want to have to explain my reluctance."

"We'll solve this." She gave him a kiss, somehow both reassuring and hot.

A little dazed, he watched her jog toward the lodge for a few seconds before taking his cell out of his pocket. It was too early to call his mom. Irritation raced up the back of his neck. Who did the film crew think they were, pulling his family into things without his consent?

He shot his mother a text telling her to feel free to ignore the request for ornaments, that he'd deal with it, and headed in the opposite direction, to Luke and Emma's cabin.

If one could call the two-story, alpine-style house a cabin anymore—after Aleja Brooks Flores and her crew had rebuilt the place over the fall, it was fit for the cover of *Architectural Digest*.

A light was on in the kitchen, shining out onto the surrounding forest. Hope against hope it was his cousin up, and not Emma. He didn't much feel like explaining the problem to his cousin's fiancée. If Bea wanted to bring her sister into the inner circle, fine, but Brody didn't want to talk about it.

His knock echoed off the surrounding trees like a woodpecker having a tantrum.

Three seconds later, the door flung open. The porch light flicked on, illuminating the concern in Brody's cousin's eyes. He was wearing his game warden uniform.

"What's wrong?"

Luke always cut to the chase, and in this moment, Brody appreciated his efficiency.

"I need your help."

His mouth gaped. "At six fifteen in the morning?"

"It's…well, it's not an emergency, it's urgent," Brody said. "We're apparently decorating a tree today. The production team tried to bring my mom into it, and you know how it is with us and trees. Do me a favor. Cobble something together from Grandma's ornaments? Or some of yours? I don't care what they are. I just don't want my mom to have to root through all my childhood stuff. If she didn't already throw them all out."

"Brody?" Emma's sleepy voice drifted from behind Luke. She yawned and ducked under his arm, leaning on him. "Aren't you leaving for town?"

Well, crap. "Yeah, in a few minutes. I just needed to ask Luke a favor."

Emma blinked, straightening. "What?"

"Don't worry about it, Em." He turned his gaze on his cousin. "Would you have a few minutes to do that? Our schedule's packed today."

"The things you do for love," Luke said, voice low.

"Yeah," Brody said.

"Or as close to love as you'll ever get," Luke said.

Emma elbowed him. "What's that supposed to mean?"

"Do you know how many times this guy has sworn to me he'd never fall in love? It's difficult to believe that'll change, even for Bea."

His heart pounded in his chest. God, Bea deserved better than what he had to give her. "That's a conversation for another day. Right now, we need someone to organize this tree debacle so that the crew doesn't find out—"

Gulp.

Emma stiffened. "So the crew doesn't find out *what*?"

"So they don't figure out they're faking." Luke shook his head and kissed the top of Emma's. "I've been telling you, firecracker."

"And you're wrong."

And Brody was going to kill his cousin for not keeping his suspicions to himself.

"Can we stay on topic here?" he said between his teeth. He could really go for sliding under the porch and communing with the raccoons who liked to hide out and plot revenge on the nest of squirrels in the closest tree.

"Brody…" Emma said quietly. "I've been telling Luke he's wrong, but…is he?"

His throat tightened. "It doesn't matter."

"Oh, I'd say it does. This is my sister's heart we're talking about here."

Ears buzzing, Brody swallowed. "Bea is my biggest priority. I swear."

"But are you in love with her?" The question whizzed past his head like a warning shot.

"I…" Damn it, he couldn't lie, not to Luke and Emma. "What do you want to hear, Emma? I don't think you'd like the truth."

To his credit, Luke didn't even look smug.

Emma, on the other hand, reeled backward like she'd been hit by a truck. "You lied to us."

"Only to keep you from having to lie *for* us," Brody said. "Without the wedding, Bea would be on the hook for a lot of money, and you two wouldn't get paid for these weeks of no guests." Bea's pride, too, but that wasn't his to explain.

Emma's face crumpled. "The wedding is fake?"

"Not at all. We're getting married."

"For how long?" She threw up her hands. "Though

I probably already know the answer to that. You might not love Bea, but you'd stick by her as long as she needed. She, though, will invariably get bored and move on."

Defensiveness rose in his chest. "Hey. She's doing this for you as much as herself. And she's not going to 'move on' from me. She's been more of a support to me than anyone has. Ever."

Emma had the grace to look at least a little sheepish.

Luke put a hand on his fiancée's shoulder and shook his head at Brody, a knowing look in his eyes.

"Don't tell Bea I found out until later," Emma whispered. "I need to think about how I want to handle this. It's a mess, Brody."

"It won't be if we can get to 'I do,'" he said. "Bea can't afford otherwise. Neither can you. But I'll let you broach the truth with her later." He checked his phone. "I have five minutes. Luke, can I trust you to handle the ornaments?"

"Yes." His cousin shook his head. "First time in my life I can say I'm sorry I was right."

"Thanks, I guess."

He wasn't about to admit that a small part of him agreed.

Bea stood at the edge of a wood-planked dock, clutching her coat lapels under her chin and shivering. Rashida was out in Hank's old aluminum fishing boat with one of the camera operators, under a blanket. Kaitlin was at Bea's side, teeth chattering. How Brody was out on the water, seemingly unfazed by the temperature, she did not understand. He was cruising across the rippling surface of Moosehorn Lake in a borrowed boat. It was nowhere near as beautiful as the wood-hulled single shell that he saved for fun rows in Seattle. Then again, the man pulling the oars was so gorgeous, the boat didn't matter.

Bea still had her heels on, and her dressy wool coat over a short flared dress and leggings, earning no end of teasing from Brody over the contrast with the fitted athletic wear he'd changed into before launching his boat.

It left no muscle to the imagination as he set a rhythm.

Pull. Pull. Pull.

Every stroke exactly the same length as the one before.

That would so be what it'd be like to have sex with him—leashed power, meted out in perfect, all-consuming thrusts.

If they got there. Would they? He hadn't been desperate for anything beyond pleasing her last night. Was he putting her off because he wasn't actually interested? Just trying to save her feelings?

"Wow." Kaitlin interrupted Bea's thoughts. Legitimate fascination lit her eyes. "You can tell he's a pro."

"I know. I've probably watched him race a thousand times. It never gets old."

But it had taken until he'd set the same rhythm with his fingers to see the eroticism of his sport.

Wow, indeed.

"Does seem like a lot of trouble for the sake of a minute of film, though," Bea said. "We sure raced through the interview at the bakery. The stroll through town square was more of a sprint." She was about ready to set fire to Rashida's filming schedule today, given the producer had refused to take the tree decorating off the call sheet when Bea had voiced Brody's and her objections to the activity.

The PA frowned. "When we have an Olympian on the show, we need to play that up."

"Yeah. I've watched his career since the first time he dipped a blade in the water. When he took his first set of lessons, I tried it, too. It stuck with him, though." Not so much her. One other pastime she'd tried and deserted.

"Were you there when he won Olympic gold?"

"Of course," Bea said. "Brody's grandpa has a whole wall of pictures, trophies and medals hanging in his place. You should ask to see it once we're back at the lodge."

"I hope you have an Olympic-themed ornament. We'd be able to tie it all together."

Bea frowned.

"Could have told you Rashida wouldn't budge on

the tree decorating," Kaitlin said. "Once something's on the call sheet, it's sacred to her."

"Mmm," Bea said.

Kaitlin's inquisitive gaze flicked from Brody out on the water to Bea shuffling in her admittedly inappropriate shoes, trying to stay warm. "Why are you two so opposed to it? You picked a Christmas wedding." The PA's smile turned sly. "Or, rather, you and Jason picked a Christmas wedding. Is that Brody's issue? He doesn't want to be the stand-in?"

Bea's neck got hot. Panic raced through her. They couldn't afford for Kaitlin to keep sniffing around. She whirled toward the other woman. Halfway through the turn, the heel of one of her sparkly shoes clunked between two of the slats of the dock. "Damn it." She tried to wiggle it free. It wouldn't budge.

"Shoe stuck?"

"Yes." And Brody wasn't going to let her hear the end of it; he'd teased her for wearing her heels this morning. Bending down, she grabbed the toe and heel and yanked. It came free.

Quickly.

Bea pitched backward. Windmilling, she caught Kaitlin's mouth forming an *O* and a flash of sky and a shout from somewhere behind her. She heard her own screech, somehow disconnected from her body.

The water slapped. Bubbles and a cold so frigid it was like falling into a flame. Her wool coat dragged at her. She kicked. Green glowed above her head. Or was that the bottom? Was she upright? Those flames, choking her, freezing her muscles. Another kick.

She tore at the buttons, thrashed for the surface.

Something clamped around her chest, dragging her toward the brighter green.

And then it was all pale gray, just for a second. Gray, and bright, and… Brody. Swearing his relief in her ear. Turning her, somehow grasping her waist and doing some sort of fancy kick that kept him upright while he propelled her onto the dock. She landed with a sucking splat of wool and a groan.

He hoisted himself up next to her and helped her to her feet.

Both her feet were bare somehow.

"M-my…m-my sh-shoes… L-lost one underwa-water…" She lifted an arm to try to get her sodden coat off—it had to weigh twenty pounds—but was shaking too hard. Water cascaded off the hem of her short dress, landing around her bare feet like a rain shower. She could see she had toes. Just couldn't feel them.

"Your *shoes*? Fricking death traps on a dock, I *told you*…" Competent fingers stripped her of her coat, freeing her from the weight.

Noise swirled around them, concerned crew members and a few people from the kayaking club offering assistance. *Is she okay?* and *Here's a first aid kit* and *I sure hope you got a clear shot*. Her vision narrowed on Brody. White rimmed his brown irises.

"H-how are y-you not sh-shivering?"

"I'm too mad."

After tucking something crinkly and metallic around her, he whisked her into his arms, lifting her from the dock and against his chest. The motion was swift, but unlike the disorientation of struggling underwater, the band of strong muscle at her back and under her knees anchored her. Icy water ran from her hair, down her neck.

"M-mad?"

"No. Not mad." The gruff retraction warmed her. So did his breath on the chilled skin of her temple. "Scared witless."

"I'm o-k-kay."

"No, you're not. We need to get you inside, in dry clothes." He glanced at Kaitlin. "The boathouse has some spare leggings and technical shirts. Grab something in Bea's size, the warmest you can find, and bring them to the women's change room."

"Holy d-dictator, Batman," Bea said. "He meant p-please, Kaitlin."

The assistant shot her the first favorable look she had in days.

Brody stood, carrying Bea with zero effort. She peeked over his shoulder. His rowing shell floated twenty feet off the dock, next to the tin skiff filled with the TV crew. "Your boat."

"Travis will deal with it."

This was ridiculous. "I can walk."

"You don't have shoes." He stormed toward the boathouse. Well, squelched, really.

She tilted her head, so close to his face it was hard to get a read on his expression beyond the granite set of his jaw. "You're overreacting."

No response. He strode into the building like he owned the place.

The club director held a change room door open. "All clear, Brody. There are a couple of towels on the counter."

"Thank you."

He set Bea down on the pristine floor of an accessible stall and turned on the water. After checking the temperature, he positioned her under the stream from the wide showerhead. Cupping her face with shaking hands, he ran his thumbs along her cheekbones. His hair was plastered to his head and his wet clothes clung to his fit frame.

"W-we need to get warm," she said. The heat from the shower water soaked into her already-wet hair and clothes, washing away the cold. "Not just me. You went under, too."

"I wasn't *drowning*."

"Neither was I."

His mouth was a firm line of *you sure as hell were*.

"Brody, chill."

"I could not be more chilled right now."

"Oh, my God, a dad joke? Now?"

"I will say *anything* if it means I stop reliving your head going under the water and not coming up again, Beatrix." His mouth slackened, haggard at the corners. Those broad shoulders slumped, and his fingers dug into her shoulders to where she could almost feel each imprint individually.

"Oh, love. Warm up with me." She pulled him under the shower and held him tightly. Rivulets of water, chilled by his cold clothes and skin, splashed her. Her hands weren't the only ones shaking. His fingers slipped a few times as he worked at the zipper at the back of her dress.

"Need to get this off you."

"And to think, not that long ago you were saying that for an entirely different reason."

He chuckled. Oh, that was a much better noise, shifting back toward his baseline instead of the serious, guarded man who'd taken over on the dock.

Freed from the material of her dress, her skin prickled under the hot spray.

"Let me just—"

The door opened.

"Oh, crap." He closed the gaping fabric back up.

Kaitlin came in carrying a stack of clothes. She dropped them on a bench. "Here. Clothes, for both of you, though I'm assuming you'll want to change into something different for the tree decorating. I'll figure that out. FYI, Rashida's rejigging our timing. Scrapping the trail ride. She doesn't want you out in the cold after having been in the water. We want to leave in ten for your parents' place. The crew'll need to set up while we deal with your makeup and wardrobe."

"We'll leave when Bea's warm," Brody said, voice barely more than a growl.

Twin feelings battled in her stomach: the comfort of being cared for, and the worry over changed plans.

"Luke might need more time to collect your ornaments," she whispered.

No doubt her sister was pitching in, too. God, she owed her sister. Nothing but support from day one. She hadn't expected that. Was she underestimating her family?

Something to ponder.

And maybe Bea and Brody could buy their family members a few more minutes.

"I'm still shivering," she said. "Can we have more than ten?"

"Like I said, we're not going until Bea is warm," Brody grouched.

Kaitlin made a face. "Be as quick as you can. Time's money today."

Wasn't that the truth. The possibility of a big old bill hung over her head today more than it had any other. And the longer she and Brody could delay, the better the chance of Luke and Emma working their magic.

Chapter Eleven

Brody was certain his heart rate would never return to normal. Screw the production—he just wanted to stand here with Bea under the hot water and monitor the pink flooding back into her cheeks.

The second Kaitlin left the room, Bea flew into action, flinging the shower curtain closed and stripping out of her dress. The fabric landed on the tile with a splat. "How are you not cold, too?"

"I am. But I'm more used to it than you." Brody's head whirled from the shift in action. "Hey, slow down."

She wobbled, struggling to push down her leggings.

"Sweetheart. *Stop.* You're going to slip. And you've

exceeded your quota for falls today." He steadied her shoulders and then knelt to strip the sodden, fitted fabric over her feet. Had she not pitched off the dock, he'd have taken full advantage of exposing all the pretty parts of her body. But she had, and his mind was tuned in to an entirely different channel after seeing her struggling below the surface of the winter-cold water.

Well, almost a different channel.

Her peach-toned underwear and bra had gone sheer in the water, and the shadows of her nipples and the tidy patch of hair between her legs did beckon a little.

Okay, a lot.

And much like last night, he needed to get a fricking hold on himself.

Her lips weren't purple around the edges, but even under the stream of the shower, the goose bumps on her arms were obvious.

"Jeez, would you get yourself warm, too, already?" She unzipped his top layer and took it off, throwing it on top of her discarded dress. Her fingers went for the hem of his shirt next.

"This was not the scenario I'd pictured for the first time you took my clothes off," he said, unable to keep the heat from his tone. He didn't know what to make of the restless feeling under his skin. Residual fear, probably.

And sheer lust.

The type of energy that usually resulted in him

seeking out a woman who was into sharing some momentary, fleeting pleasure. Just enough to take the edge off.

He'd been hesitant to treat Bea that way.

But if we're going to do this for the whole time we're married, that's not fleeting.

The corner of her mouth tilted, and she skimmed her palms over his pecs. "You sound so certain I'm going to strip you down."

He brushed a wet hank of hair off her forehead, tucking it behind her ear. "Might have been early when we left this morning, but there was no mistaking how wistful you looked when I got dressed."

"Arrogant much?" She hooked her thumbs in his waistband and pushed it down a few inches. Then a few more.

She took his underwear, too, shoving them to his thighs. Her mouth got perilously close to his crotch as she knelt to free him from his layers.

He groaned, unable to stop himself from getting half-hard. "Are you seducing me in the shower, Beatrix?"

Still kneeling, she shot a playful look at his exposed length and then up at his face. "No. Anyone could walk in. Hell, they probably will, to nag us to hurry up." She bit her lip and stood, a scant finger's width of space between them. Her wet underwear brushed his arousal, making him even harder. "On the other hand, I *was* thinking we could stall. Help out your cousin."

"Oh, altruistic, then."

"Exactly."

He palmed her stomach. "I can think of some altruism."

"Does it involve us trying to delay our location change?"

The skin of her stomach was tantalizingly soft.

"It involves me locking the door."

She shifted her hips against his, the friction heating him from the inside out, stealing the last dregs of cold that had settled in his bones when he'd dived into the frigid water.

Her teeth scraped her bottom lip. "You should do that."

He did, bolting to the door and back as fast as he could.

In the shower again, he tried his best to get every inch of her front against his naked self.

"So." He dug his fingers into the plush globes of her ass and aligned their hips. "Stalling."

"Yeah." Her hips circled. "Stalling."

"I prefer the idea of savoring."

"I could go for that instead." She gasped. "Or both."

"I've always loved your insistence on taking every last bit of pleasure from every moment of the day."

A blink of doubt, and then she served him with a slow, sensual smile. Her hands looped around his neck. Soft lips landed on his collarbone. Nipped his throat, the crook of his neck.

"I need to taste you again," he said.

He knelt at her feet, ignoring the hard slate of the floor and propping on his heels so that he could bury his face between her legs. Goddamn, she tasted like a dream. Salt and sweet. The smooth skin of her thighs and the soft patch of hair… Enough to make a man's head spin, if he let himself fall under her spell.

He couldn't do that, but he could make sure he shorted out every one of her senses. Kissing her mound, her inner thighs, parting her folds with one thumb and licking her center—purposefully ignoring her clit until he felt her relax.

She whimpered, clutching at his hair, sagging a little.

Excellent. Pretty sure he'd made her knees buckle.

Well, he could do even better than that.

"Quiet, there. Door's pretty thin," he warned.

Her next moan was muffled.

He glanced up. She was biting the back of her wrist. *Holy hell.* He moaned himself.

"Damn, you're hot." He mouthed her tight bud, open, then closed. Feasting on her, taking on more of her weight with a hand under her ass as she whimpered and groaned and got wobbly. Water sprinkled and splashed him every time she shifted and wiggled.

"Brody, I was supposed to do this to you next."

"No rules here, Sparks."

A lie. There were definite rules. Though none about how many times he could earn that breathy gasp.

"You're not supposed to be this good at this…"

"Why?" he said.

"'Cause I'm going to want you to do it again."

"I'll do it anytime you want."

Spending a year doing this... He could get on board with that. Could get addicted to coaxing her toward bliss.

Tasting her body gave him as much of a high as plucking her from the frigid water of Moosehorn Lake had been a low. His head was still spinning from the shift.

Tension settled in his core, but he resisted the urge to take himself in hand. The urge to bury himself in Bea's softness, really, but he didn't have a condom, so he wasn't going to suggest that.

Her hands tightened in his hair.

"Close?" He thrummed his tongue against her sweet center.

"Too...*mrph*."

"Too much?" He eased off, glancing up and taking in the red flush in her cheeks, the close-to-coming twist of her mouth that would have looked laughable if it didn't signal he was a few tongue flicks away from making her dissolve.

"No... Too *close*. Want it. Can't quite—"

He thrust two fingers into her wetness. It had worked last night. So slick, so soft. He hummed his own pleasure, feeling his balls tighten.

"I'm going to... Don't let me fall... *Oh!*"

She pitched forward a little, her hands gripping his shoulders.

He wrapped his forearm around the backs of her thighs and held her up, the joy of her release washing over him, too. Her inner muscles tightened around his fingers. A wild moan filled the air.

That sound. It was the ultimate peak, and it roared through him, insistent, brilliant. Life-giving. He came, spending without even having been touched.

Had that ever happened?

But something about having Bea like this—why was it so different?

Bea sat in the back of one of the large SUVs the production team was using to transport cast and crew. Her cheeks were still heated and most certainly pink. She was pretty sure she and Brody had been quiet enough to go undetected. Maybe everyone else would assume her blush was from the hot shower.

She knew it was from Brody ruining her for oral sex with anyone else in her life.

Weirdly enough, the thought of being intimate with anyone but Brody seemed the definition of wrong.

He sat next to her, ignoring the local scenery zipping by outside the windows as he checked something on his phone. Oblivious to her inability to think about anything but when they'd next get the chance to be alone. Describing her impatience as a need to "return the favor" wasn't quite right. It wasn't a favor. It was about care and excitement and release. All things she was eager to give to him.

"Have you heard from Luke?"

He nodded, eyes fixed to his screen. "He's sending something over with Emma."

"Okay." Bea might've been warm in her borrowed rowing attire, but it wouldn't do for filming. Emma was meeting them at the ranch with extra clothes. "What about your mom?"

Concern creased his brow. "Haven't heard a word."

Rashida turned in the front passenger seat. "Kaitlin talked to your mom yesterday. She's supposed to meet us for the tree decorating."

"I heard," Brody bit out. "And I told her not to. Mom wouldn't be comfortable on camera."

"We need the emotion and the Christmas connections," Rashida said.

"We'd rather focus on our future Christmases, not our past ones," Bea jumped in, heart thudding at the bent truth. Aching a little, too. They'd spend this holiday together, but by next year, it would be back to Bea celebrating with her family and Brody eating Christmas Eve lasagna with Hank.

"You know us." Rashida grinned. "We go for sweet, not drama. But I have to thank you, Brody. That was some real hero business out on the water. Enough that I can't stay mad over how damn long the two of you took in the change room."

Bea's stomach twisted the rest of the drive. Ten long minutes later, they pulled up to her parents' house.

Her jaw dropped. "Oh, my goodness, they hung the Christmas lights early."

"They were only too happy to festive the place up when we asked if they'd be willing to host the tree decorating." Rashida's eyebrows knit together.

Of course the producer wouldn't understand why Bea had expected her family not to buy into the wedding-related activities.

Though they've all been supportive, except for Mom.

Was she being unfair, assuming they would view the event through the Bea's-a-screwup lens they'd so often used?

Someone knocked on her window, and she jumped.

Emma held up a pair of shoes.

Bea opened the door. *"Thank you."*

"Of course," her sister said, flinging her arms around Bea. "I was so worried when I heard what happened."

"Imagine what it was like watching it," Brody grumbled.

"Oh, honey, I bet," Emma said, a strange, suspicious look crossing her face.

"What's that look for?" Bea asked.

Emma paled. "Oh, nothing. Uh, Luke got a few ornaments from Hank, but when he called his aunt, she told him she was already planning to come."

All that stall tactic for nothing? Bea sighed.

Well, not for nothing. There was that whole ruined-for-future-sex part.

But...

"Brody, your mom's on her way," she whispered.

"I'll talk to her. Make sure she knows she doesn't have to participate." Brody squeezed Bea's hand.

Rashida's gaze fell on their joined hands. "I can tell you're nervous, feeling awkward. And it's not hard to tell why."

Bea's heart jumped into her throat. "Rashida, I can explain."

Except she couldn't really, not without screwing up absolutely everything.

Rashida waved a hand. "Nothing much to understand, Bea. It took falling out of love with one man to see you were in love with another. And now you're planning a dream wedding and trying to make sure that your family is on board with what is admittedly a sudden change. It's overwhelming."

"Oh, you...you saw all that." *Bought it.*

"Of course I did. Not hard to see the way the two of you exchange looks like you want to give each other the world."

Kaitlin snorted.

Rashida swatted her. "None of that from the non-romantics in the crowd, please and thank you."

"It... You're right," Bea said. What else *could* she say?

By the time they were walking down the path, her stomach was ringing an alarm. About what, exactly, she didn't know. With Emma serving her funny looks, and Brody feeling protective of his mom, she couldn't help but feel the afternoon was doomed to go the way of the rowing footage.

"Hey." Brody was right behind her and put his hands on both her hips. "Since when do you catastrophize? Where's my relaxed, go-with-the-flow Bea?"

Her feet landed on the first stair to the porch, and she turned to face him. "How do you know I'm catastrophizing?"

"You've had worst-case-scenario written on your face all day."

She didn't want that, didn't want to be in that mind frame and have it show up in the footage, or have him think she was upset. She lifted a shoulder and tried to look eager.

With him a step below her, they were essentially face-to-face. He kissed her, slow and easy. "I don't like that smile, either. You don't have to force happy with me."

One of the things she loved about Brody. The problem with being Miss Happy-Go-Lucky was people didn't like it when she experienced an emotion more complex than joy. She'd never had to do that around Brody. He saw her ugly sides.

He *loved* her ugly sides.

And she loved him for that.

She loved *him*.

Full stop.

And not just as my best friend.

Her knees started shaking, and she stared into the bottomless brown of his eyes. Was she really realizing her true feelings for him while standing on her parents' front porch, in the midst of the crew bustling to and fro, getting ready for the next filming?

"Hey," he said, stroking her face. "Seriously, what's wrong?"

"Why would you think something's wrong?" She was only setting herself up for certain heartbreak come the end of their temporary relationship. No big deal. Nothing to worry about. And definitely nothing she'd ever tell him.

Chapter Twelve

Bea looked so miserable, he signaled to Rashida to give them a minute and leaned in to give his fiancée a hug.

She stiffened and scooted up the stairs backward. "We should get inside and— Oh, there's your mom."

An ancient—but somehow still immaculate— Pontiac pulled in next to Rich Halloran's blue F-350.

Brody had stopped asking his mom why she was still driving the muscle car. The thing was murder on a tank of gas, and she had an ongoing tab with a local mechanic. He knew, though. She'd drive it until it was impossible. And she'd never get rid of the twenty-year-old air freshener hanging from the rearview mirror, long faded from red to pink.

Bea paused in her retreat, waved at his mom and called out, "Hi, Cammy!"

His mom made her way along the path to them, carrying a small box, wearing a parka and a nervous smile. The wind caught her chestnut hair, blowing the straight strands around her face. Her brown eyes, which were the only physical trait she'd passed down to Brody, were bright. A good sign. Maybe she was better rested and in a healthier space than the last time he'd come home. She'd been having a rough go with her depression at the end of the summer.

Hopefully today didn't nudge her into one of those dark places.

Her gaze flitted to the camera crew, who was getting set up along the gravel path and wood rail fence for the outdoor shot of Brody and Bea carrying the Christmas tree into the house.

"Couldn't have given me a little more time to shop for a dress, kiddo?" she said lightly.

"When you know, you know."

"I sure do." Corners of her mouth turning down, she gave him a hug, then shifted in her winter boots. "Am I going to have to be on camera?"

"Not if you don't want to be."

"I'll think about it." She held out the shoebox. "Ornaments. Thought you could use them today."

He took the box, confused. "I thought you got rid of the Christmas ornaments."

"Not the ones you made," she said, crossing her

arms. She took in Brody, and then Bea. Pain filled her eyes. "Marrying your best friend. Just like me."

Not just like her at all. He wasn't going to fall in love with Bea. Wasn't going to risk driving around the same car for twenty years.

She backed up a step. "You look really busy. I'll get out of your hair."

"Wait, Mom." He didn't want her to stick around and feel uncomfortable, but he didn't want her to leave, either. With him living in Seattle, they got so little time together, and he'd been occupied since he got to town. *Candidate for best son of the year here, folks.* "Can we have lunch or something? I don't think the crew needs me the next couple of days while Bea's making the rest of the flowers."

She smiled fondly. "I'm working the next two days, hon. I'll see you for your tux fitting on Friday, though. I've been asked to join you for that."

He couldn't help but feel a bit disappointed as she left. He didn't expect her to fill the role of two parents—that would be unfair—nor was he surprised she wasn't jumping for joy that he was getting married. It was just the ongoing regret, the reminder life hadn't been normal since the day they found out their family of three would forever be a family of two.

He threw himself into filming, pretending to be eager for the event.

"Wait, you want me to drag the tree up the drive?" he asked Rashida after she got them set up to bring the tree into the house.

"Can you carry it over your shoulder?" she asked.

A few of the crew members nodded as if they'd seen her make similar requests in the past.

"They're going for the burly lumberjack look," Bea whispered, stifling a laugh behind her fist.

Her laughter prickled. He wasn't used to wanting her approval. Not in that way.

That prickled even more. "You'd think, after I managed to pull you from a lake, that you'd have more faith in my tree-hauling abilities."

"Oh, I'm sure you'd look spectacular."

Her cheeks flushed.

His went hot, too.

Out of the corner of his eye, he saw a circular lens. Great, more fodder of him looking sheepish over the attraction he felt for this woman.

It shouldn't. He should have been happy that he'd looked far gone for her. Except that was too close to actually falling for her. It wasn't for the cameras. It wasn't to be shared.

Hell, it wasn't for him to experience at all.

This was acting. That was it.

But he wasn't much for hauling the tree in single-handedly, either.

"We should do it together, Sparks," he suggested. "It's our thing."

Her slow grin rolled over him like a victory. She positioned herself at the tip of the tree. "Well, I'm sure we could *both* carry it over a shoulder."

He hoisted the trunk as she did the same with the top.

They walked the tree into the Hallorans' country-chic living room, laughing as they secured the monstrosity in the stand.

Soon after, they stripped off their outerwear and got their makeup touched up while a PA hung the tree with lights. Four boxes nestled next to the tree, one on top of each other in wedding-cake formation.

"You know, the best thing about decorating a tree is that you know exactly what's in the boxes, but it feels like a surprise to open them, nonetheless," Bea said, clearly for the benefit of the camera. She winked at him.

She still had her arms crossed.

"You cold?" he said quietly.

"I'll warm up once we start moving."

Screw that. Shaking his head, he went to the wood-burning fireplace and quickly built a blaze on the grate.

He turned. Bea sat next to the tree with the box from his mom on her lap.

"Should we start with this one?"

He didn't even have a proverbial Band-Aid to rip off. Not anymore. It had been on so long, it was fused to his skin. Grown over. This was just tearing off a chunk of himself, leaving an open wound.

And it wasn't something he could open up about now, not while the camera was focused on them, ready to capture the nostalgia of the holiday that only represented pain and frustration. The reminder he hadn't been enough or done enough to pull his mom out of her grief.

Families celebrated holidays after the death of a loved one all the time. Even through the pain. Most people managed to love without it ruining the season. Even managed to find goodness after horror. But a handful of people, like his mom, loved so deeply that the end was soul-wrecking. And if he let himself love Bea, would he turn into that?

She sat on the floor, face glowing with that internal light of hers. The one that so often cast beams into his own dark places. Dimmed only a fraction by the silent question on her face—*Are you ready?*

He'd have to fake it, like he had been every other time this week.

"Open it up," he said, sitting cross-legged on the throw rug covering part of the wide-planked floor.

"Are you sure?" she murmured.

"Let's see what's in there. Been a while since I've looked at them."

She flipped open the top, which bore streaks of dust his mom had clearly tried to wipe off but hadn't been able to bring herself to finish the job. A layer of tissue paper covered the memories beneath.

Bea plucked at it tentatively.

He'd seen her open boxes and presents many times. She dived in like an eager kid.

Not with this box, though. She held it like it contained a priceless Fabergé egg.

Or maybe a pissed-off king cobra.

He took it from her and dug in. Enough of being afraid of pom-poms and pipe cleaners held together with decades-old Elmer's glue. The few Christmases his dad had been home, he'd hung Brody's ornaments first, making sure they occupied a place of honor on the front of the tree. Once the branches were sagging from the weight of all the decorations, Brody had sat between his parents on the couch and they'd all admired their work. He'd soaked up every second of his mom's contentment and his dad's warmth and the evergreen scent, knowing how finite the moment would be.

This thing with Bea—equally finite. Equally precious.

Protective paper coddled each ornament individually. He grabbed the biggest one, about the size and shape of a baseball.

"This one reeks of 'My First Christmas' energy," he joked, the words creaking in his throat like a rusty swing set.

He peeled back the wrapping, revealing a ball wrapped in satin thread and hugged by a thin plastic strip, emblazoned with a stork and his predicted message.

Bea seemed to shake off her concern and reached for the smallest box behind her. "I have one of those, too! They must have been on sale somewhere in town in the early nineties."

She dug through her own box until she unearthed

the same ornament, identical but for "Beatrix" and her birth year in small gold letters under the stork.

Laughing, they hung them side by side on the tree. Someone in the crew let out an "aw."

Rashida hushed them. "This is good stuff here. I want to get it with the initial reactions instead of having to cut and reset."

"What else do you have?" Bea asked him. "I doubt you can beat this one. My best five-year-old work."

She revealed a cross-eyed Frosty the Snowman, with one pipe cleaner arm shorter than the other and a mouth painted on with Joker-esque lack of precision.

"I knew pom-poms and pipe cleaners would be well-represented," he said, poking around in his own box for something equivalent.

She laughed.

"Aha!" he said. "Here!"

He passed her a beaded snowflake that must have earned him an F in elementary school art. Globs of glitter formed grotesque stalactites. His lack of talent earned another tinkling laugh.

He reached back into the box, closing his hand around a long, thin ornament. *Oh. This one.* His heart panged—his grandfather had always tried to make the holiday special, especially when Brody's dad was deployed.

"What's that?" Bea leaned toward him. Her hair fell in her face and she pushed it back.

She missed a strand.

He caught it with a finger and tucked it behind her ear. "You'll love this one."

Brody passed over the miniature hand-carved rowing shell—a replica of the one he stored at his rowing club in Seattle. His grandfather had glued strips of wood together and then carved it by hand to mimic the larger craft they'd made together.

"Oh…" Bea cooed, examining every inch of the small carving. "We should put that up on the shelf in your—the living room. Year-round. It's beautiful. Look at the detail…"

The detail. The only one *he* could focus on was the one where she'd be living in his space. It had seemed an easy suggestion at the beginning.

Would it be possible to be easygoing with Bea in the future?

Breath coming too fast, he fumbled in the box and pulled out the next paper-wrapped object. It was light and…

Faded red. A cardboard tree, edged in glitter. Once upon a time, it smelled like wild cherry.

He'd painstakingly painted the edges and dunked them in silver sparkles, given it to his mom one Christmas when it was just the two of them. That last one. "So he can be here, too, Mom."

He never was again.

Brody's throat closed over.

Goddamn it. Why was it you could go through life completely fine, and then at an unsuspecting moment, grief slid in and broke your oar lock, dumping you into the frigid past?

"What's that?" Bea asked.

He held it up, sending her a silent plea.

Her eyes widened a fraction. "No way, you still have that?" She reached for it with a shaking hand. "I mean, I made them for everybody one Christmas! But my parents threw theirs away. Claimed it blocked out the scent of the real tree."

Another lie, but it gave him enough time to clear his throat without having to resort to a huge hacking cough.

"You always have had a way of adding glitter to something ordinary."

She frowned.

He winced internally.

Too much, Emerson.

Though it was the truth. She added something special no matter where she was.

Specifically, to his existence.

And he couldn't lie to himself anymore—getting married was going to mean more of that glitter, in a different way. Once he had that in his life daily, would he be able to let it go?

Luke slapped Brody on the shoulder and sent him a sympathetic smile. "I'd welcome you to the chaos, cousin, but you're not new to this scene, nor are you sticking around long."

"Right. Uh, has Emma decided to talk to Bea

about it all yet? I don't want to keep it from her for long."

"They'll figure it out in their own time. You know how they are," Luke said.

"I know Bea puts more stock in what her family thinks of her than they realize," Brody said, taking a pull from his beer. He scanned the crowd in the Hallorans' living room, now decked with a Bea-and-Brody specific Christmas tree and, blessedly, no cameras. Bea's little brother, Graydon, played with his infant twins on a blanket on the floor. Jack held court on the couches with Nora, Bea's parents and Brody's grandfather. Emma flitted around, refilling the trays of food on the coffee table and sideboard, throwing come-hither glances at Luke.

After one particularly heated, silent exchange, she yawned wide enough to fit the barn.

Brody pointed the neck of his beer bottle at Luke's fiancée. "Em looks like she wants to hit the hay. Either for a nap or to take advantage of you. Hard to say."

"Both, likely. Been a long week for more than just you and Bea."

"Nice you two are doing so well." A year ago, the two had been neighboring rivals who were anything but neighborly. He hoped against hope the pair would beat the odds.

"You're getting to be a pro at changing the subject," Luke said.

"What, about me not sticking around long? Nothing to say."

Luke scoffed and lowered his voice. "You're marrying a woman you've been telling me you don't have feelings for—one I'm pretty sure you're sleeping with—and you have nothing to say?"

Brody raked a hand through his hair. "We're not sleeping together."

Yet. They'd probably go there tonight.

Luke lifted an eyebrow.

He took a breath, fighting off his annoyance at his cousin poking the bear. "What is there to say?"

"I dunno. Admitting you're in love with her?"

A record-scratch of a statement. "I can't do that, Luke."

"You're not *not* in love with her."

He closed his eyes. "Since when have I ever been capable of being in love with someone?"

"It's not about being capable or not being capable." Luke's tone was as gentle as Brody had ever heard him use. "It's about letting yourself be vulnerable, deciding to put in the work."

"Christ, have we lowered ourselves to talking about being vulnerable?"

"That's toxic crap and you know it." Luke frowned. "Don't think you believe it, either."

He hung his head.

Luke rested a hand on his shoulder again, to squeeze this time. "Just be open, Brody."

Talk about asking the impossible.

Emma sidled over. "This looks like a conversation that I need to be a part of."

"Not particularly," Brody said cheerfully.

His sister-in-law-to-be grabbed both his and Luke's arms. "We need to find Bea. Away from everyone else."

At least she understood the importance of that. Luke and Brody stumbled in Emma's wake as she strode into the kitchen. They found Bea there, fussing with a flower arrangement on the butcher-block island. She'd changed into jeans and a casual T-shirt after filming. Still looked stunning.

"Come," Emma ordered, face set in determination. She nodded as if to say, "And that's final," making her ponytail sway.

Bea's eyes narrowed. "Why?"

"Call it an intervention."

Brody groaned internally. He was not in the mood to get reamed out, even if it was deserved.

"Figure it out in their own time?" he said under his breath to his cousin.

Luke lifted a shoulder and followed his fiancée out onto the porch. "Firecracker, we talked about this."

"No, you talked at me for a bit." Emma flicked on the propane heater under the covered area and waved a hand at the two outdoor couches. "Now it's my turn to talk to *them*."

Bea sat, staring at her hands in her lap. "Go ahead. We deserve it."

Brody took the space next to her and put an arm around her shoulders, pulling her in close and rubbing her back in as comforting a gesture as he could manage. "You're not going to talk us out of this, Emma. And we'd really appreciate your discretion."

"Talk you *out of it*?"

"Shh, Em. Someone's going to hear you inside," Luke said, pulling Emma with him onto the other couch. Scratch that, onto his lap. The two of them couldn't be more stereotypically in love.

He really hoped they knew what they were doing.

"But..." Emma's green eyes darted from him to Bea, who still wasn't looking up to make eye contact. She poked her sister with a toe. "I'm not going to talk you out of making Brody your groom. I get why you did it."

Bea finally looked up, a kernel of hope brightening her cheeks. "You do?"

"The money," Emma said. "And I'm betting your pride, too. When I found out this morning, my first reaction was to chalk it up to you constantly changing your mind about things."

"Emma," Brody warned, hating the way Bea's cheeks went pale.

"No, no," she continued. "I realized that wasn't fair. Because of everything in your life, you've never quit Brody. Which—" her smile turned eager "—don't you think that means something?"

"No, I don't," Bea snapped, springing to her feet.

"We'll be able to stick with each other because we're *not* in love," Brody explained.

Bea let out a strangled sound. "Not sure what promise I want from you more, Ms. Matchmaker—for you to keep our secret, or butt out of our very platonic relationship."

Very platonic? Bit of a stretch there, given how many orgasms she'd had in the last twenty-four hours. By Luke's snort, he wasn't buying the descriptor, either.

Emma didn't seem to clue in, though. "I'll... I'll of course keep your secret, but, Bea—"

"Stop, Em. Please." Crossing her arms over her chest, she strode off, down the quarter set of stairs and into the dimly lit backyard.

"Crap. I'm sorry, Brody."

"She'll cool off," he said. "I'll follow her. Make sure she doesn't take off." He left in the same direction as his pissed-off fiancée, a quiet chorus of nickering horses and Emma lamenting her failure to Luke at his back.

"Bea?" he called, taking the path around the side of the expansive farmhouse. "Beatrix?"

She didn't respond, but it wasn't hard to find her. She was leaning her forearms against one of the fences, staring off into the distance at one of the grazing herds.

Rounding behind her, he nuzzled the top of her head and cupped her lush hips. "Gonna miss dinner if you're not careful."

"Not really hungry."

Damn it, he'd do almost anything to make it so she wasn't hurting anymore. He'd tried, anyway. But their solution seemed to be making it worse.

"I'll leave you to it, if you want some peace and quiet."

"As if this house is ever peaceful or quiet. Especially with my siblings around, eager to wedge their noses where they don't belong." She rested her palms over the backs of his hands and rocked on her heels, pressing her shoulders and bottom against his chest and the fly of his jeans. She sighed. "I shouldn't be too hard on Emma, though. At least in one regard, she's willing to stay quiet."

"I guess. She should respect our boundaries, though."

She snorted. "Even though we aren't respecting them ourselves?"

"I dunno," he said, dropping his lips to the side of her neck. Her skin was pure perfection. Would he ever get enough of kissing it? "I like the new ones we drew."

They were alone, with no need to put on a show for anyone. He still wanted to touch her, for the sheer pleasure of it. Hopefully to earn a quiet gasp—just enough to know his hands sent her head spinning as much as being near her made him dizzy. He skimmed his fingers closer to her belt buckle.

She spun in his arms to face him. "Next time we do that, it's about you."

He was tempted to lift her onto the top of the fence and kiss the breath from her. "How long do you figure it would take for someone to come looking for us, to catch us?"

Nimble fingers played up the back of his neck. "Catch us doing what?"

"Whatever you want."

"Not sure when we'd get caught, but we'd definitely end up missing dinner."

"As much as I like your mom's cooking and your dad's chocolate cake, I could live without it."

A rueful smile crossed her face. "If only."

"Later."

He expected a laugh, but instead she went serious.

"What's wrong?" he asked.

"Nothing's *wrong*, but… Is it…is it about more than me being glittery?"

"What do you mean?"

"Earlier. You said I had a way of taking something ordinary and making it glitter. Or something like that. And I…" Her fingers tightened on the back of his neck. "Being glittery isn't enough, Brody. I want to have substance. To matter."

She didn't think she mattered? How could anything he'd done this week have suggested anything *but* her mattering?

"Bea. Sweetheart…"

"You don't need to scramble to fix it. I know how people see me."

"Clearly, you don't. Because if you said something

like that, it means you don't understand that—" he cradled her cheeks in his hands "—that sometimes… sometimes I think you're the best part of my life."

A tiny gasp escaped her lips. Green eyes flew wide open, her long lashes fanning at the corners. "Brody…"

The best part of my life.

He couldn't take it back.

Not when she needed to know it.

Not when it was true.

"Hey!" Graydon's voice boomed from the patio. "Lovebirds! Time to join us in the living room for the shoe game."

"We'll finish this later, okay?" he said quietly.

The kissing, anyway. With any luck, she'd leave her examination of his feelings be.

Chapter Thirteen

"Later" dragged out longer than Bea would have thought possible. The stupid shoe game, practice for their big day. Kinda cheating, but who wanted to get that kind of thing wrong on national television? Dinner itself, delicious but seeming like it had eighteen courses. Her sister, acting equal parts weird and like a matchmaker.

All throughout, wondering what the hell Brody had meant by what he said.

By the time her mom and dad declined her offer to help with dinner clean-up, telling her to go spend some time with her fiancé, she was downright itchy with the need for Brody to elaborate.

She fidgeted the whole car ride back to the lodge

with Luke and Emma. Once they said goodbye, she grabbed Brody's arm and pulled him toward their cabin. With the crew off having free time and no outside guests around, it felt like they were the only people on the lodge property. Wind blew through the trees, cold against the back of her neck. Even though she knew she was warm, she'd been fighting off the mental chills all day. She couldn't wait to get under the covers with Brody. Partly for the warmth, partly to finally show him how she felt.

"It's later," she pointed out.

He followed, a dazed look on his face. "Yeah, and?"

"You said we'd finish our conversation later."

Was that a groan from him?

She glanced back, but between the dim lighting along the path and his ability to make his face as blank as could be, she couldn't tell.

Frustration rose as she hurried down the rest of the path and led the way through the front door. The cozy cabin air warmed away the November chill. The fire-lighting elves had visited again, ensuring a fresh blaze crackled behind the glass. "Was it okay for me to claim I made that ornament today? I didn't want you to have to talk about your dad."

"No. That was a good cover, to make it seem legit."

Believable on the surface, but with that edge of sadness… Regret ground in her gut.

"I'm sorry this is dragging up things you left long behind you."

Though maybe he hadn't left them behind.

He took both her hands and spun them around. Leaning back against the door, he pulled her between his legs, against his chest and open jacket.

Warmth surrounded her. The fire in the grate, heating the air to a toasty temperature. The circle of his arms, the comfort settling in that if he was upset, he wouldn't be holding her.

She rested her forehead against the soft cotton of his shirt. "There are so many things coming up that I hadn't anticipated dealing with."

"No kidding," he muttered. He hooked his fingers through the belt loops of her jeans and held her in place.

"Everything's a thing today! The lake, the tree… and then what you said. What you *said*." She palmed his chest, dragging her thumb between his pecs. "I'm used to our routine of supporting each other, no matter what. To knowing I'm important to you. But you've never suggested I was *that* important. Or what meaning I should be reading into that."

"It's not about reading into it." His hoarse tone sent shivers up the back of her neck. "You're my best friend. And sometimes, I realize that means you're one of the best things in my life."

"'One of'? Earlier, you said 'the.' *Sometimes* 'the,' that is."

"Yeah. *The*." With a groan, he captured her face in his hands and her lips with his own, kissing her until she could barely think about anything, let alone semantics.

Keep a clear head.

"We have the backbone of a supportive relation-ship. Add in this..." She deepened the kiss, just for a second. The closeness, the rightness of it all. "Are we that far off from a real marriage? We have most of the parts of a relationship."

"Minus a willingness to commit," he said.

Not on my part. I love you.

And tonight, she'd show him.

Raking her gaze from his messy mop of hair to his well-built thighs, Bea bit her lip in a last, desper-ate hope she wasn't about to make a fool of herself. She walked backward, pulling him along by a hand-ful of his shirt.

"What does that look mean?"

"What do you want it to mean?" She sat on the bed, face so, so close to the crotch of his jeans.

"Things I shouldn't." His voice pitched even lower, thrumming through her like a bass line.

"Why shouldn't you?" she said. "We're adults. We get to make our own rules."

The tip of his tongue darted out to toy with his bottom lip. Oh man, he was that nervous?

He sat next to her and met her lips with his, half kiss, half moan.

Snagging her behind her knees, he pulled, throw-ing her a little off-kilter.

She landed on his lap. *Yeah, that's right.* His hard length teased her through thick fabric.

His fingers slid to her hips, his thumbs drawing tantalizing patterns through her jeans, stroking her hip bones. The fire was warm at her back, but nothing to match the inferno of his flesh against hers, even with their jeans on.

"Hang on," he said.

Damn, was he having doubts? Wanting to pause?

She was about to ask why when he slid his fingers under her bottom and stood in a swift blur of strength.

She squealed, tightening her legs around his lean hips and gripping his broad shoulders. "Oh, *literally* hold on."

"Well, yeah. It'd be bad form to drop my bride four days before the wedding."

"Rashida would lose her mind if we threw another delay at her."

His mouth tilted. "Let's leave all of that behind for tonight. It's just you and me, exploring something new."

He laid her down on her side of the bed and joined her, looming over her like every dominant fantasy she'd ever had. Her head spun, tipping toward overwhelmed, but this would be okay. Her body clamored to be closer to him. Her heart demanded that, too. To get the chance to show him they could be vulnerable together and they'd be safe.

"I love exploring new things." Hands greedy to

discover everything about his gorgeous body, she flicked open the buttons of his shirt, exposing a delicious expanse of tanned skin, a sprinkle of golden hair and ab muscles that shouted "doing sit-ups is part of my job."

She looped a calf behind one of his thighs and pulled him against her. His erection was as hard and glorious as the rest of him. She intended to enjoy all of it, to make sure *he* enjoyed it. To tell him wordlessly that he was her most important person, too.

"You totally sure about this?" His lips curved against her collarbone, and he licked a hot trail from one to the other. "You know the world tells us that friends shouldn't sleep together."

"Well, the world can piss off. We're the ones who get to decide what does and doesn't work for us."

That hot mouth crept down, kissing all the way. "And this works for you, Beatrix?"

"It would work better with less clothing." She pushed his shirt from his shoulders and tossed it aside.

"See, quick like that is great, but something about slow is even better." Rising to his knees, he knelt between her spread legs and teased her T-shirt up above her navel, gazing in appreciation at his work.

The air chilled the exposed strip of skin. A shimmer of goose bumps. Even more with the brush of his lips, a slow, sampling taste along her belly.

She shifted with impatience. To go from him cradled at her center, all that hot promise he'd fill her every need, and now to lose that pressure—her body cried for more.

Later. First, she needed to explore him. She pushed him onto his back and tasted her way down his chest, his belly. Her fingers fumbled, shaking on his belt buckle. The fabric resisted her attempts to slide it down until he finally lifted his hips, groaning his assent.

"Exactly," she said, gently gripping his length and giving him a slow stroke. "You want this, right?"

"Yes," he rasped.

She took him between her lips, his aroused flesh smooth and hot under her tongue. "Yeah, I want this, too."

The salt of him, clean and earthy, melded on her tongue—the taste of Brody so clearly defined. She'd never forget it. Nor how it felt to have his hips rising as she licked and caressed, thrust and teased. He strained in her hand, and she took as much as she could, smiling around his length every time he muttered her name in the most reverent tone she'd ever heard him use.

"Sparks..." His hand landed on her head. "I don't want you to stop, but you gotta."

"You sure?"

"Yeah. I want more than this."

"If you insist." She rose on her knees and prowled up the bed.

"This way," he commanded, rolling them over. He chuckled as he nudged her shirt off. An eyebrow lifted a fraction, and he traced an imperceptible fingertip along one of the candy-cane stripes of her padded bra. "Festive."

Resting an elbow on the mattress, he lounged next to her, tangling their legs together and cupping one of her breasts with a roughened hand. His thumb outlined the edge where white-and-red satin met sensitive skin.

"Spoiler alert, it's a matching set."

"Mmm, something to look forward to." Deft fingers flipped open the front clasp. The fabric fell to the sides.

"Bea..." His head lowered, tongue flicking her puckered nipple. She clutched his shoulders, arching into him. He feasted on her breasts. Desire cascaded through her, settling between her legs. His hand drifted to rest right above her mound.

"Undo my jeans." She barely recognized her voice through the rush of blood in her ears.

He lifted his head from his ministrations, grinning and cupping the back of her head, kissing her gently. The hand on her belly slid farther down, pressing her aching core through annoyingly thick denim.

Biting her lip to suppress a moan, she clutched his hair with both hands. She closed her eyes, bringing his forehead to hers, pressing her pelvis against his curious fingers. "Seriously, Emerson, the zipper."

A controlled breath brushed her cheek. "This one?"

The waistband loosened with the released button.

Then a rasp of metal teeth. And his touch, dancing past the trimmed triangle of hair she liked to keep for moments like this because damn, the friction was irresistible.

Light friction. Just one fingertip on either side of her sex. Driving her so close to breaking that she was almost afraid how good it would be when he entered her.

"Brody…"

He parted her folds and nestled a rough digit at her entrance, pressing in just far enough to earn a whimper.

"What do you like, Sparks?"

"Anything's good. I'm kind of…kind of… I just… I need this. But more. Deeper."

His hand thrust, burying two fingers like she asked, and pleasure raked her like a private sunset. A precursor. She didn't want to come yet. Wanted to feel that with him.

She gripped the sheets and let herself fall into the heaven that raced through her veins, sent there by his skillful fingers. "You…" A wave tossed her closer to the peak. "It's… What, have you been training for this moment or something? Because—" his finger curled and sent her into herself and out again "—that's too good."

"No such thing."

"There is when…" His fingers, working in her wetness, brushed a spot that made her vision tunnel.

Humming in obvious satisfaction, he rubbed it again.

She moaned.

"When?" he asked.

"When I don't want to finish yet. I want to come with you."

"Nothing saying you only get one orgasm." He sounded so damned sure of himself. She'd allow it, given he was turning out to be as gifted with her in his hands as he was with an oar.

"I know." She reached down and cupped his cheek, tugging up in a silent message to pause. "I still want to share that. No matter how temporary this is, it's special."

"Very." His agreement rasped from his chest. It promised he'd prove it.

Reaching for the bedside table, she pulled open the drawer to display the ceramic sugar-packet holder with over a dozen condoms tucked inside it instead of servings of pink and blue sweetener. "Someone seemed to assume we'd need some. We're fully stocked."

"I don't even want to know which one of our relatives did that, but then, I guess I should be thankful," he said, peering at the stash. "More than supplied."

She plucked one out and held it between two fingers. "Or just enough. Be a shame to waste any of them."

His eyebrows rose and he fumbled to take his

pants off one-handed. "You're so sure we're going to want to do this again?"

"Why wouldn't we?" She stripped off his underwear, pausing as she took him in. Brody defined "feast for the eyes," and she had no qualms enjoying the chance to catalog his strong body and how clearly eager he was to be in bed with her.

She stroked her palms along his chest. His erection lay on his thigh, beckoning her to slide her hands down farther and caress his hot length again.

"Yes?" she asked, an inch away from taking him in hand.

A garbled plea.

"Told you you'd want more." Satisfied, she pumped her hand as slow as she could. She loved coaxing the wild noises from his throat.

"Keep doing that and you're not going to get what you want," he said.

"What's that?"

"Put the condom on me, Bea."

That face, that goddamn familiar-as-her-own face. Inches from hers, filled with passion. Dropping sweet kisses on her cheeks and lips.

She put the condom on him.

He lined up, blunt head nudging her folds. God, she was wet. In another life, her responsiveness might have made her blush, but tonight, it only meant extra pleasure. Her body clamored for the promise written in each caring touch, in his hungry gaze.

And when he thrust, filling her deeply, it overwhelmed. Sparks and pressure and her racing pulse. Him, every inch of him touching her, moving against her burning skin.

Covering her.

Completing her.

She met his thrusts, a primal rhythm. It was the best feeling she'd ever had. It still wasn't enough.

"Brody." She knew she was thrashing under him, losing control. Searching for that elusive completion his body promised.

Slick skin and hard muscles and those beautiful brown eyes.

Too easy to fall into those eyes. She was in the circle of his arms, protected, cherished, so close to tipping into bliss.

Another thrust.

"Bea, sweetheart." His jaw clenched in the very best way. He was trying to hold on for her, make it good.

"Touch me," she whispered.

His fingers slipped between them, nestling between her legs. Gentle, roughened, perfect. Matching the rhythm of his hips, teasing her slick flesh. Sweet nothings rode his lips, fervent vows to take her anywhere she wanted to go.

"I don't know." She moaned. "No, I do. Take me... Take me with you."

"I will. I want to make you feel..." Another tick of his jaw, hint of a smile on his lips and in his gaze. "Everything."

Hooking her calves around the backs of his thighs, she pressed against his hand, needing the pressure on her mound, just enough to make her vision narrow and her blood rush in her ears. Pleasure shimmered at her core. He circled his thumb, rasping against her bud.

"Yes, I—" She tipped into white-hot release, no longer out of reach. Brody's weight was on top of her, yet she flew through space.

He groaned. Time held, only passing through gasping breaths and racing heartbeats. His forearms braced on either side of her head as he kissed her temple, mouth spread in a wobbly grin.

She held him, drifting like a leaf in the breeze. He was still thick inside her.

"We're not getting any sleep tonight, are we?" She spoke into his shoulder, moving her lips along his sweat-slicked skin.

"We probably should, for tomorrow's sake. You have a lot of flowers to deal with."

"Not yet. Haven't had enough of you."

Would she ever? In another world, one where he actually liked being in a relationship, this could feel like exactly what she needed: not for a year, but for the rest of her life.

Chapter Fourteen

A bead of sweat trickled down Brody's neck. Partly from the heat of the portable filming lights set up in Dreamy & Dapper, Sutter Creek's formalwear store, partly from how damn fast the last two days had gone. He hadn't had much to do yesterday or the day before given the flowers had occupied Bea's whole schedule. They'd had their nights to themselves, though. Reveling in pleasure they'd ignored and repressed for so long. How it got better each time, he didn't know, but he wasn't complaining.

Today, it was work first, fun later. His hours were packed. The fitting, and then the rehearsal.

My wedding rehearsal...

He smiled shakily at his mom, who was participating in the suit appointment.

"Talk to each other!" Rashida prompted from behind the lights. "Memories. Hopes. Dreams. All the good stuff."

Memories. Yeah, that wasn't happening.

"Kinda unreal I'm getting married tomorrow," he said, keeping things bland.

His mom straightened his tie for the camera. "Bea's everything a mom could hope for, honey. She puts a sparkle in your eye."

"That she does." *Being glittery isn't enough.* Her words from a couple of nights ago still nettled him. "If I do one thing as a husband, it's going to be to make sure she knows she's valued. The parts she lets everyone see, and the ones she keeps hidden."

The director yelled cut.

Shoot. Right. That had been on film. It was so weird to have his intimate thoughts captured.

"Was that not enough?" he asked.

"It's fine," Rashida said. "The tailor will do the actual fitting now, and we'll meet you back at the lodge for the rehearsal. We need a head start to set up."

The crew bustled to pack their gear and left Brody on the menswear side of the store.

Once the tailor deemed his work perfect, he left Brody and Cammy.

She patted Brody's lapels. "You look just like your father."

He winced. "Sorry."

She drew back. "Why? I can't think of a better man for you to emulate."

"I hate that you get this sad look in your eye sometimes. When you look at me."

"Not because it's hard to look at you." As if on cue—the sad look. "Because it's hard to see you grown and accomplished and that he never got to see any of that. He'd have loved this, you know. You marrying your best friend."

"Yeah?"

"For sure. Always the romantic, your dad. I never thought I'd see you in your own wedding. But it suits you."

What the hell was she saying? The cameras were off. It was just the two of them. She didn't have to pretend to be okay with him getting married. "You're not going to warn me off?"

"Why would I?"

Disbelief surged, hot and bitter. "Mom. I had to throw away one too many uneaten meals and encourage you to take a shower ten too many times to believe you support this."

Her smile wobbled, but it was genuine. "I'm okay being alone, honey. I'm not going to say I'm happy all the time, but as long as I take my medication and go to therapy, life feels like it has meaning. I'm not the ball of out-of-control grief you lived with."

"I'm glad you got help. But watching you go through what you went through…"

The regret on her face looked deep enough to reach

to her marrow. "I'm sorry you had to take care of me instead of the other way around. I did the best I could, but it sure wasn't enough for you at that time. Thank God you had your grandfather and your coaches to watch over you during those years."

"And Bea."

"And Bea," she echoed, her smile turning knowing. "I'd have seen it then, had I not been so actively dealing with my depression. Or not dealing with it."

As much as it had involved so much pain, he understood her reaction. Giving Bea his heart and losing her would ruin him. "I get it. Dad's death—"

"His death didn't cause my depression. I just lost the will to manage it." She squeezed his hand. "Took me a while to figure that out. I wasn't able to properly put in the work until I did. And I'm proud of you for overcoming the fear of loss in a way I've struggled to do."

But he hadn't, though. If he had, he'd be committing to Bea for real tomorrow.

Bea fidgeted with the makeshift bows-and-ribbons bouquet her mother had hung on to from the bridal shower they'd held months ago. Good thing she'd listened to superstitious warnings about not starting to use any gifts given to her and Jason— she'd be able to return them easier once she was back in Seattle.

"It feels weird to use something connected to Jason," she whispered to Georgie, tucking her coat tighter around her for the outdoor rehearsal. It was the first time she'd thought of him in days. Yikes, that was telling... It allowed her to detach from his connection to the riot of plastic and satin in her hand, too.

She looked out over the rows of chairs to the lake beyond. A breeze teased the glassy surface and ruffled the tops of the towering evergreens lining the other side of the bank. The forecast for tomorrow was for sunshine, so it was full steam ahead to hold the ceremony in the wedding clearing overlooking the lake. At the end of the grassy aisle, the handcrafted arbor, Luke's work, awaited her approach.

Her mom shrugged. "It would be weirder for you not to have a ribbon bouquet at all. They're family tradition."

Tradition went beyond the tacky cascade she carried. It seeped into the very dirt of the area. Bea's grandparents had married in this clearing, and Emma and Luke planned to follow suit once her sister finally managed to narrow down what she wanted her ceremony to look like.

Her sister and Luke wouldn't have cameras everywhere, though. The rehearsal was currently delayed ten minutes while the camera and sound crews fine-tuned the setup. Brody, his cousin, his grandfather and a coworker from Seattle whom Brody had paid the airfare to come and join the wedding party all stood at the other end of the aisle, joking around while they waited for things to start. Her cousin Jack, too, who'd gone through the rigamarole of getting ordained online so that he could officiate. Not far from Bea and Georgie, Emma and Nora waited with their dad and Lauren, one of their cousins, her oldest daughter in tow. The preschooler had been only too happy to step in as flower girl once Jason's niece was no longer involved.

"Speaking of tradition, I'm confused," Georgie said. "What happened to you wanting to walk down the aisle *with* your fiancé? You swore up and down since you were a teenager you wouldn't get Dad or me to walk with you. Every time Emma waxed poetic about her ceremony, you were intent on marching to your own drum."

Truth, every word of that. She'd always pictured walking toward the altar hand in hand with her husband-to-be, just like they would approach life.

She lifted a shoulder. "That wasn't going to fly with Jason's family."

"But you're not marrying Jason, honey," her mom said gently.

"I know." Not so gentle. She winced at her tone and smiled in apology.

"Which we're thankful for." Georgie stroked one of Bea's shoulders. "As unconventional as your timeline has been, your father and I are so happy for you and Brody."

I wish we deserved that happiness.

Tears sparked in her eyes.

Alarm crossed her mother's face. "What? You're not having doubts, are you?"

She shook her head. "Not at all. Brody and I need to do this."

"That's a strange way to word it."

"I know. I—" She couldn't lie anymore. She'd have to trust that she and Brody could figure out what to do if learning the truth lost them her parents' support. She glanced at the crowd nearby and pulled Georgie away, to the far side of the back row of chairs. Bark mulch crunched under her feet, half the speed of her racing pulse.

"Beatrix, what's going on?" Georgie asked.

"It's not real, Mom."

Her mom sat in one of the chairs. Wind buffeted them, sinking into her bones. Nothing could feel as cold as the disappointment on her mother's face, though.

"You're *not* getting married?" Georgie whispered.

"No, we are, but…"

"Wait. Your dad needs to hear this, too." She waved at her husband. "Rich!"

He must have picked up on the alarm in Georgie's tone because he hurried to join them.

Bea checked once more to make sure they were alone and unheard. And she spilled. Every last ounce of it, minus the intimate parts. Those didn't affect her parents.

Her parents' faces crumpled.

She deserved that reaction.

"You lied because of *money*?" Georgie asked, standing.

"Yes. Ensuring my shop didn't go under. And making sure Emma and Luke's lodge didn't lose weeks' worth of income. I wasn't going to ask you. I know as much as anyone that the ranch is surviving by the skin of your teeth—no fault of your own, of course, but… Anyway. This was our only option to salvage my contract."

Her parents exchanged one of those no-words-needed looks shared by people who'd been married forever.

"No, honey. Not why you lied to the studio folks. I can see your reasoning, even if it's kinda wacky. You didn't need to lie to us, though."

"It seemed easiest. Avoiding you all having to lie for me." She swallowed down the lump in her throat. Today was not the day to get into everything ugly and raw underlying her decisions. If she cracked open, she wouldn't be able to close up again. Would ooze her issues all over an event people were expecting to be bliss-soaked.

Rashida would lose her mind if it turned into a drama fest.

"Easiest." Her mom's lips were flat. "I'm not going to pretend to be thrilled about this—"

"Neither am I," Bea said.

"And quite frankly, I was looking forward to having Brody as a son-in-law."

"You will. Just not for as long as you might have hoped."

Georgie sighed and traded another long multitudes-in-a-second glance with Rich. "We'll go along with it, honey. I've no wish to embarrass you. If you honestly think this is the best decision, the only way to get you where you need to go, we'll stand by you."

Bea's jaw unhinged. "You will?"

"Yes. However unconventional it is. We're used to unconventional with you."

"And I've always felt lesser for it," she blurted.

Her parents wore twin stricken expressions.

And Bea felt so light after finally admitting the whole truth, she nearly tipped over when a gust of wind whipped around them. She gripped her mom's elbow for support. Eyes shining with tears, Georgie covered Bea's fingers with her own.

Her dad ran a hand down his beard. "You always barreled through. Pushed forward."

"No point in being stagnant," she said.

"Always thought it was the Halloran stubbornness, just a unique angle on it," he said. "But...was it a defense mechanism?"

"What?" Wait. Her dad saw her stubbornness and drive as making her more a *part* of the family?

"I could be way off," he demurred.

"No." Letting go of her mom, she rested her cheek against her dad's chest and ringed her arms around his burly torso. "You're right. It always seemed more productive—more fun—to soothe myself with another adventure, with something new, than to obsess about how my baseline wasn't enough."

"I wish you'd said something." Georgie winced. "Sorry. No. That's the wrong take. It wasn't up to you to point it out to us. All your talk as a teenager about wanting to get out, not feeling like you fit. I thought that was typical teenager stuff. I didn't realize it had stuck with you."

"Hard to see that when I'm off all over the country," Bea said, her words muffled by her dad's sport coat.

"That's generous of you to say, but this is on us, honeybee," Rich said.

"Relationships are a two-way street. I know that." *Why things won't work with Brody in the long term: Exhibit A.* "And given I've had a lot of these feelings as an adult, I could have spoken up. At least found peace, if not understanding."

He stroked her hair. "We were in awe of you. Nervous for you. Downright scared sometimes. It's not easy to know what to do with a kid made of stardust when you're built with soil and sand."

Stardust. Brody had always seen that in her, reveled in that part of her, never tried to brush it away.

She glanced at the other side of the clearing, where he was doing an on-the-fly interview with Mark. God, he was handsome, comparatively dressed up for the outdoor rehearsal in a button-up shirt and dress slacks with a charcoal wool coat for warmth against the clear November day. The coat was open.

He had his hands jammed in his pockets, which lifted his broad shoulders a touch. Combined with his wide smile, he looked carefree, a hint of awkward in that super sexy way. The "this isn't comfortable, but I'm going for it" thing—it turned her on, every time.

She stepped away from her dad.

Her mom rubbed her back. "You're looking at Brody differently this week."

"I know."

A truth never so obvious as a half hour later, holding his hands in front of the altar. His grip, as strong as the nails and screws holding together the weathered wood of the arbor. Luke had built the structure over a decade ago and fixed it up for Emma's new wedding-lodge adventure. The cables of winter greenery Bea had twined together looked perfect draped over the rustic branches.

Focus on that. People were going to see her work. Her business was going to flourish. A ton of folks would want to get married in this same place. It was falling into place.

And you've fallen in love with Brody.

How was she going to come back from that?

Would having a business be worth it if her friendship fell apart?

"All right." Jack's no-nonsense direction broke through her thoughts, though not through the dread making her stomach rigid. He had a clipboard of notes thicker than the instruction manual she'd had to memorize as a theme park princess. She should be leaning on that more, really. The poise, the glitz, pretending everything was a fairy tale. "Once Bea makes her way up the aisle and you're both here—"

"Wait," she said. "I want Brody to walk up the aisle with me."

Brody's hands tightened on hers. He lifted an eyebrow.

"I've always wanted to do that," she explained. "Because I'm not meeting you at the altar. We're walking toward it together."

"We are," he said, solemn.

"Color me surprised you want to change something," Jack said cheerfully. "Hence, I brought a pen."

She winced at his jab. "We don't have to."

"Yeah, you do," he said. "Of course you do. Change it a million times if you need to. Make it perfect."

Jack's tone was light, but something in his gaze caught her. Was he annoyed? Or maybe it was something about his own fiancée, Paisley. It was odd that she was coming to the wedding at the last minute.

Bea glanced down the aisle. Tomorrow, a long runner would cover the wood chips. "Can we try that?"

Jack waved a hand at the far end of the aisle. "Fill your boots."

They repositioned, Brody on Bea's right, the warm strength of his hand still grounding her.

"You should walk the same speed as when you did it yourself, Bea," her cousin called. "That looked good."

"Didn't know you were the expert," she teased.

"Do you know how many wedding videos I've watched on YouTube? I bet I could give Rashida some lessons."

Rashida, standing behind the camera with a few of the crew members, rolled her eyes. "Stop making boasts I need to cut."

Jack saluted her with two fingers and motioned for Brody and Bea to start walking.

She'd been nervous the first time she made this journey. With Brody at her side, it was somehow easier and more nerve-racking, all at the same time.

He measured his strides to her shorter ones.

She looked up at him.

A faint hint of unease marred his fond, confident gaze.

You okay? she mouthed.

"Of course," he whispered back.

It sounded like the truth. But if he was having doubts...

They stopped at the front row of chairs. She gripped his hand, forcing him to look at her. "Are you sure?"

He stroked her cheek with his free thumb. "Couldn't be surer."

All things people would say to each other if they were both madly in love and ready to take on life together.

Skating his thumb across her lower lip, he winked.

Her breath caught. Her thoughts followed, stuttering, getting hung up on that wink, on his touch.

"That's not on script," Jack interjected. "Though I'm sure the camera loves it."

"You stick to what's on that page and let me decide what looks good on film, yeah?" Rashida said.

She wanted to hug her cousin for his clear attempts to keep things jovial. The weight of the lie, the weight of what a wedding should have meant but this one *didn't*, bore down on her shoulders.

Jack pulled a pair of reading glasses out of his pocket, put them on and peered at his notes.

Bea laughed. "Way to call back to Poppy Halloran," she said.

"These are all mine," he said.

"Get it all out before tomorrow, I guess," she said.

"Dearly beloved… Nope, that's wrong." He flipped a page. "Mawage is what…" Another page.

She chuckled at the reference from *The Princess Bride*. Brody shook his head.

"You know, I'm going to surprise you with my intro," Jack said. "But that'll be first, and then I'll read the declaration of intent you gave me."

The words they'd so casually tossed together a night ago, while tangled together in bed.

"Maybe we should just follow the traditional 'richer or poorer, sickness and health' spiel," she said. All these personal touches…perfect for making things seem real.

So perfect that she craved that reality.

She wanted to be here, doing this with Brody, and didn't want it to end.

Could she hide that from him for a year? Go through with the revered words and promises, knowing they had an agreement, knowing that the year they'd agreed to would never be enough?

"Let's stick with what we've got," Brody said.

"If I get two cents," Rashida called over, "listen to your groom. It's beautiful and will play better."

Bea let out a breath. "Okay. Unique, it is."

"Good," Jack said. "Then it's vows and rings, I pronounce you two kids as married, and we walk down the aisle and proceed to eat our weight in Yorkshire pudding bites. Easy peasy."

"Right. So simple." Strain flooded into her tone before she could stop it.

Jack shot her a sharp look of concern.

Brody kissed her cheek. "We got this, Sparks. We're okay."

Would he still be saying that if he knew how much she meant every word scribbled on the page in Jack's clipboard?

Those words hung around her like a cloud for the rest of the evening, weaving through the whirl of the rehearsal dinner for their extended family and closest friends.

When her cousin Cadie pulled her aside to share congratulations, her "marrying your best friend is the only way to go" advice blended into the opening of Bea's vows. *I loved you when you were "just" my best friend. I love you even more now.*

Or her uncle's "you two have had *forever* written

all over you since you were kids." She smiled weakly at that one, sipping from her champagne and trying to block out the *I can't wait to see how much I love you in ten years. Twenty. Fifty.*

Why had they gone so over-the-top?

Her hand shook, and her glass of champagne almost slopped onto the artisan-milled flooring. She'd been here to help lay the planking of the newly renovated great room. Each of the rough wood boards weighed what had seemed like a metric ton. And right now, it was like they were all pressing on her chest. She took a deep breath, struggling against the constriction.

"Speech!" Emma, holding a plate covered in cake crumbs in one hand and looking entirely too gleeful, dinged her fork against her glass.

Oh goodness, there was no way. Panicked, she scanned the crowd for Brody, finally finding him on the other side of the buffet table with his cousin. She sent him a silent plea.

Nodding, he called out, "We're saving the words for tomorrow, Em!"

His voice carried through the groups of their friends and family standing and sitting around the five round tables scattered with the remnants of their meal. His refusal earned a few friendly boos and an orchestra of forks tapping on glasses.

They weren't getting out of this without at least a kiss.

He motioned for her to join him.

She wove past his grandfather, her dad, a few of their friends from Seattle who'd been invited when it was her wedding to Jason and were happy to come—though somewhat teasing—despite the groom switch. Everyone claimed they weren't surprised at all. She couldn't tell if they were being honest. Could they all see it? How much she'd lost her heart?

"I can't," she whispered to Brody, grabbing his hand.

"I know." He kept it just for her, murmuring it into her ear. He lifted his glass and raised his voice. "I know everyone says they're the luckiest person in the world the night before they get married. And I see what they mean now. Thanks for sharing this with us. Might have been a surprise for some of you, but that's life with Bea, right? It's what makes it great. And I can't wait for whatever surprises she has in store for me. To my bride!"

Everyone echoed the toast.

All Bea could hear was the loop of Brody. *Whatever surprises she has in store for me.*

How about that she loved him? She doubted he'd want that dumped on him. Not now, not a year from now.

But she had to. She couldn't go through with the ceremony without him understanding how much her feelings had changed. If she said those vows tomorrow, she'd mean them. And he needed to know that, before he recited them back to her.

"Brody…" She gripped his arm. "Before I head to my parents' we should—"

"Beeeeeeea!" Emma swooped in, crinoline skirt swishing and heels clicking and painstakingly pinned curls not moving an inch. "We're taking you away. You can see him in the morning."

"No, he and I need to—"

"Nope! Bridesmaid veto. It's time to go to the ranch."

Brody let go of Bea, gaze locked on hers. "I'll see you tomorrow, Sparks."

He leaned in for a kiss.

Something so simple.

It melted her, every time.

But it obviously wasn't the same for him, and that imbalance—it wouldn't work. Their friendship could survive it—he wouldn't make it weird—but it would be dishonest not to be clear. She couldn't afford to hide things with Brody like she'd done with her parents and siblings.

"We really need to talk," she said.

Emma's green eyes widened. "Bea. You've had a big day. I know." She almost sounded panicked. "But you have a plan for tomorrow, and you can figure out the rest later. Okay?"

No, not okay.

"Your sister's got a point," he said gently. "Go have a good sleep. Can't wait to see you all dolled up tomorrow."

Yeah, still not okay. But with him resisting and

Emma tugging her away, she wasn't going to make a scene.

She'd find a time to tell him how she felt in the morning.

Of course, come morning, there was a camera on her every second.

She had to pretend getting her hair and makeup done wasn't agony.

"Those wedding-day nerves are killing you, huh?" Emma asked, eyes flicking toward the camera positioned on the other side of the living room in the ranch house. It had seemed like the more intimate place to get ready. Now it just felt miles away from Brody.

She lifted her hands. The makeup artist working on her false lashes hissed for her to stay still.

"You just love him so much and can't imagine a moment without him?" Emma was clearly describing her own life.

But it applied to Bea, too.

"Yeah," she whispered. "He's my everything."

And she wasn't his.

Nora stared at her sharply.

Her mom, still in a robe but in full hair and makeup, came over and squeezed her hand.

"You know how it took so long for you to tell Dad and me how you feel?" her mom asked. She leaned in and whispered the next part. "Don't wait so long with Brody."

Advice she needed to take *before* they said "I do."

Unable to move her face for the person blending in her mascara, she waved a hand in Rashida's direction. "I need to go over to the lodge early."

"How about…no?" Rashida said. "No ruining the reveal moments."

"I want five minutes with him. That's all."

"And you can have that. When it's time to see each other for the first time."

This would be easier if Rashida was a heartless Hollywood caricature. Someone in it for the money alone, who didn't legitimately love her show and want to prove she could buck the tawdry trend.

Bea could be morally upright like that, too. She could get the words out. *Rashida, I wasted your time, and now I owe you more money than I can afford—*

How would that help anything, though? At this point, she'd be screwing Rashida out of an episode they'd been working on all week. Once they were over at the lodge, she'd insist on her five minutes alone with Brody, and they'd figure out a way to get through the day without messing up the show entirely.

Somehow, she survived the next hour of getting into her dress, sliding on her shoes, wiggling into the limo.

They'd set up the nook off the dining room as the place he'd see her all dressed up for a private moment.

Well, as private as it could be with a camera operator, a lighting tech and a very impatient host pushing her in his direction.

His back was to her, his attention somewhere out the window. A striking, handsome figure framed against the evergreens and river view. Black wool had never looked so good.

She wanted to walk into a room and greet him as her person for the rest of her life. Into the kitchen, seeing those strong shoulders flex as he washed dishes. The bedroom, rising and falling as he snored through a nap. The bathroom, glistening with water from the shower...

Her hands shook and she almost stabbed herself with the pin of his boutonniere.

Simple, Bea. Follow the script. Say hello, exchange a romantic look, pin on his eucalyptus sprig.

"Brody?" Her voice shook, too.

He turned. His jaw dropped. He covered his gaping mouth with a palm.

Didn't say anything.

Which was okay—she had enough to say for them both. Camera, no camera, it had to get out. Now.

She strode toward him on unsteady legs, stopping close enough to catch the scent of his bar soap. At eye level with lapels and buttons and a perfectly knotted tie.

"Brody, I... I understand if you don't want to marry me, but... I need to tell you."

A troubled frown drew his eyebrows together. "Sparks, what—"

"I love you." She stared into his beautiful brown eyes and finally, finally told the truth. "I'm *in* love with you. And I couldn't say 'I do' without you knowing."

Chapter Fifteen

"Cut. *Cut*."

Rashida flapped around the camera operator like a blackbird, dramatic sleeves fluttering around in her shock.

No way could the host's shock be halfway close to the stunned numbness that had overtaken Brody's brain.

If only he could call cut on what had actually just happened.

Had Bea purposefully said that on camera? She had to have. She knew it was filming and that their mikes were hot.

But then, why would she have worded it like it was a discovery?

Why would she have said it at all? She didn't love him. She couldn't.

He pulled Bea closer and lowered his head to try to create some sort of privacy. "Why did you say that? On camera? They can't use that footage, and now Rashida is going to figure out—"

She took his hands. Hers were clammy. Her eyes were a little wild. "I don't care about the camera or Rashida or the show. I care about you, and being honest with you. Nothing that we were doing here was honest, except for between each other. I can't lose that last shred of integrity, Brody. Can't have you marry me without knowing what you're really getting into."

"Wait. You meant that? That you…you…" He couldn't get the words out.

"Of course I meant it."

Something cracked in his chest, oozing helplessness and yearning and all the things that could be, were things different. "But I can't—"

He wanted to. God, it was awful seeing her put it on the line, knowing he wasn't able to do the same. The feelings were scratching at the door, but he couldn't trust there wasn't a monster on the other side, something uncontrollable that would eat them up and spit them out.

"I know you can't." Bea was calm, placid almost, as if she'd survived a kayak ride over a waterfall and was floating safely down a suddenly lazy river. "That's okay. It's not what I'm asking you for."

It was in no way okay.

"What in the name of Chris Harrison's left nut is happening right now?" Rashida thundered. "Are you telling me you've been lying to me? There was no instaromance? No big realization of being in love with each other?"

"Yes," Bea said simply.

Rashida swore.

"I told you so," Kaitlin muttered.

"We only lied about being in love," Brody said. Someone had to salvage this fiasco if Bea wasn't willing to. He wasn't throwing away their efforts because she'd let the emotions of the week get to her and started believing their fake love was something real. "She's wearing my grandmother's ring. We're getting married. We're all set up to live together after the fact."

"And then you'll divorce or something?" Rashida spat out.

"Or something," he said. "Eventually."

A hand clamped around his. The one sporting a very sparkly ring picked out by his grandfather to commemorate a forever love. Christ, what had they been thinking, using that ring under false pretenses?

"Brody, I was serious," Bea said.

He looked at his fiancée, his best friend, the woman he couldn't live without but couldn't live fully with. "I'm serious, too, Bea. Emotions are high right now, and who knows what either of us are feeling? But what matters is that we get married today."

"But you can't," Rashida said.

Brody and Bea jerked in her direction.

"Correct that. Get married all you want, but without you both being in love with each other, it's not going to be on my show."

"Is she coming back?" Bea asked, pacing the small nook for the thousandth time. The beads of her dress clicked every time she turned.

Kaitlin shrugged, following Rashida's orders not to let Bea and Brody out of her sight. She seemed more interested in snacking on a bag of Cheetos she'd somehow procured than keeping the peace.

"You're going to wear out your shoes before we even get to the aisle, Beatrix," Brody said from his perch on the couch.

He'd already made a mess of his tie and had moved onto fidgeting with the box that held their wedding bands. Even when she tried to talk to him, he kept his gaze on the floor, wouldn't look up.

Was he that upset about her confession?

Fair enough. She wasn't going to ask with Kaitlin listening to their every word, though. One major confession with an audience was more than enough for one day.

The door to the outside flew open. Rashida entered, eyes blazing and scarf blowing in the wind she brought with her.

All Bea could envision was an invoice with a giant Funds Owed total, a closed sign in Posy's front window next to the flowers-and-script logo Bea had painted by hand.

And worse, the humiliation of having to explain to her extended family and friends why there would not only be no *DIY I Do* episode, but there wouldn't be a wedding at all. Why had she assumed they'd be able to pull this off?

"I should have just paid the bill and canceled," she said under her breath to Brody.

Rashida's eyes narrowed. What Bea had initially interpreted as fury looked more like pain.

Another cramp tightened her chest. Not a heart attack or anxiety—just plain shame.

"I know it's not enough," she choked out, "but I'm sorry, Rashida. I took your work and treated it like a joke. All for the sake of my pride. I understand if we need to cancel and I'm on the hook for the costs stated in my contract."

"It's too late to cancel. We need to have some semblance of a wedding today, or else I won't be able to deliver a finished project on time. Even if I was able to find a different wedding to shoot on short notice, the costs of this show go beyond what you would owe. And I can't afford to pay those, either. So we need to set aside hurt feelings and asshole behavior and get this done. As long as you and Brody legally marry, you'll have fulfilled the terms of the contract. And despite knowing it's a lie, I will be able to make magic out of it, like I always do. I'll hate it forever, but I'll do it."

"But how are we going to go through with it now? With so many people knowing it's not real?" *With Brody knowing it's very real for me.*

"You were prepared to do it all week. I don't see what's changed." Rashida's voice was hard.

My feelings. But no, she couldn't prioritize her feelings anymore. Her putting her feelings first had caused all this chaos.

She lifted her chin and gazed into the face of the man she loved more than she'd ever loved a person in her life. "I can't ask you to go through with this."

"Yes, you can. We need to finish what we started." He took her hand, leaned toward her ear. "You deserve my honesty, too. I can't return that 'I love you,' not the way you meant it."

"I expected that when I said it." Didn't stop her insides from twisting like rusted scrap metal on a junk heap. "I couldn't go through with the ceremony without you knowing my feelings changed."

He nodded slowly. "Not surprising that one of us would catch feelings at some point. It won't change anything."

It already has.

But she couldn't fix that, any more than she could expect him to alter his outlook on love. At least they had an entire year to recalibrate now that she'd thrown them off-kilter.

She looked at Rashida. "You need us to have a ceremony."

"Yes."

"A real one," Bea clarified.

"I don't care what it is at this point, as long as I get enough shots to make it look like you love each other." Rashida's tone was wooden. "But yes, if you want to avoid legal action, you'll need to file your marriage license."

"We do love each other," Brody said quietly.

"I don't have a problem with platonic love, but it's not what I'm selling," Rashida said.

"We can make it seem real," Bea promised. "That was our aim all along. We'll shoot all the scenes that you need. The processional, the vows, the rings, the kiss…" Oh, God, the kiss. Somehow, she'd get through kissing her best friend with him knowing how she felt about it and her knowing how he *didn't* feel about it. Great. Just spectacular. Summoning all her willpower, she made eye contact with him. "We'll have the ceremony, and then we'll go back to our normal. Just friends. Not roommates. No way am I holding you to living together for a year. We'll end the marriage as soon as we can."

He served a death blow to his carefully styled hair by raking a hand through it. "But—"

"This is better." If she smiled any wider, her face would crack. "Rashida gets what she needs to finish the show. I don't owe the money. Emma, Luke and I still get to build our businesses. And you don't have to pretend to be happy about doing something you swore you'd never do."

"I promised you…"

She stroked a hand down his cold cheek. "It's okay. It's not your fault. You don't owe me a romantic relationship. And I love you too much to put you through something that's making you miserable."

"A year with you would not be a hardship."

"Maybe not," she lied. She knew the reality of it. Living with him while she felt like her heart was trying to climb out of her chest would be the ultimate in torture.

Rashida made a noise of protest.

"Like I said, we'll do everything you need to get on film," Bea assured her. "But I deserve… I deserve to be loved fully. By everyone. My family, and my partner."

"I *do* love you," Brody said, face crumpling.

"Not that way. Which, like I said—you don't owe me that. But it's time *I* accept *me*. Accept that I don't have to pretend. I am who I am. And it so happens right now that I've fallen in love with you. So, the absolute worst thing I could do for me is live with you, keep pretending. I'll find somewhere new to call home. It'll be totally normal."

Normal. As if. But she had to keep telling herself that, if she was going to be able to get through what she'd promised to do.

Chapter Sixteen

I love you. I'm in love with you...

Bea's declaration buzzed like a swarm of wasps in Brody's thoughts, drowning out the instrumental of "A Dream Is a Wish Your Heart Makes" they'd picked for the processional.

He'd never understood the phrase "I could feel their eyes on me" better than he did in this moment, hand in hand with Bea and walking down the outdoor aisle. The Hallorans' forced smiles. His mom's sad one. Emma, beaming hopefully. Not to mention the bemusement of their friends from Seattle, still believing that Bea and Brody had admitted to being in love and had decided to get married within the span of a couple of weeks—God, the reactions when they actually explained the whole situation.

Though—how would they explain?

We needed to get married to finish the show. Then Bea actually fell in love with me.

And I... I had the chance to love the best woman I've ever known, and I let it go.

No. He wasn't letting her go. They'd still be friends. Safe.

And he'd always know he hadn't been enough for her. That she'd taken the risk to confess her feelings, and he'd fallen short in being able to do the same.

What if he hadn't? If he'd been able to say "I love you, too," and walking down the aisle with this woman's hand in his was truly stepping toward a future?

For a second, he could almost see it. But then he saw his mom's nervous expression.

It tethered him to his past, to the knowledge that if he let himself feel what Bea was feeling, it could end up ruining him.

And losing her now wouldn't ruin you, wedding or not? "I love you," or not?

He shoved the question away, smiled at his mom and waited for Jack to invite them to the altar.

Jack started into his greetings and introduction. It teetered on the line between soppy and irreverent and would have been perfect for an actual wedding. Hopefully the other man wasn't too mad when he discovered all his efforts were for naught.

Bea's cousin being pissed off by his wasted effort was the least of their worries.

If they got through the next fifteen minutes, no fuss, no muss, things could go back to normal.

The laughter in his head drowned out the end of Jack's carefully crafted spiel.

Bea beamed up at Brody, every inch of her mouth curved into the perfect princess smile she'd been trained to hold for hours. Upholding that veneer of happily-ever-after, the illusion that after the theme park gates closed and everyone went home to their imperfect, painful lives, the magic lived on somewhere.

God, he didn't deserve this woman.

And yet, she still wanted him.

Jack started in on the ceremony. "These two love-birds need to declare their intentions. Join hands."

The smile tightened, just enough for him to see.

He hated that he was making a joke out of what should have been something wonderful for her. When it was both of them lying, it hadn't seemed a mockery. But now it did. She was having to stand up here and say things she might actually have meant.

Things that would have led to a life together. Wasn't hard to picture some of that. His mind spun with a kaleidoscope of the future—colors and sounds of a life that could have been. Actually decorating the tree together. Enjoying the Seattle breeze while jogging on his favorite path around the lake. Maybe one day having to temporarily slow to walks, if they were lucky enough and she got pregnant. Teaching two little humans with mops of blond curls and brown eyes to scull.

His heart ached for it.

He'd never let himself consider it, admit he wanted it.

Damn, he wanted it.

Even if he lost it. Even if it destroyed him. Having it now, having it for however many years he was blessed to have it—he *wanted* it. The now would be worth whatever happened in the future.

"Brody, do you want to marry Bea?" Jack asked.

They'd gone with the simplest wording possible. He was finally able to give a simple, truthful answer. "Yes. Absolutely yes."

The emphasis drew gentle titters from the crowd.

Didn't seem to affect Bea, though. Her face stayed locked in faux-joy mode.

He squeezed her hands. With needing the filming perfect, he couldn't deviate from their script.

Much.

When it came time for vows, he kept his notes in his pocket.

She went first, promising to always look for the next adventure, and adding a humorous nudge about letting him have first crack at the coffee maker because no way would she be getting up at 5:00 a.m. to join him rowing. She paused, smile wobbling. She bit her lip, clutched his hands and took what sounded like a breath deep enough to last an hour. "Of all the people in the world, you're the one who's always been okay with me being me. Which makes you the perfect person to spend my life with."

If only you'd get your head out of your ass, her gaze said.

I have. Promise, his silently returned.

She stared at their shoes.

He tightened his grip on her hands. *Look up, Sparks.*

"All right, Brody, your turn," Jack said.

He took his own massive inhalation. "The first time you asked to be my friend, I wanted you to go away."

Her eyes widened. "Where are your notes?" she hissed.

"I don't need notes to help me explain how I feel about you, Beatrix." He kept his voice low for that, before pitching it louder to reach the back row. "You came around, wanting me to join you on a treasure hunt. Took me far, far too long to realize the real treasure is you."

He'd said it for the cameras earlier in the week, but nothing could be truer.

Her smile stayed fixed. Her breath picked up, though, the beads on her bodice glinting in the sun as her chest rose and fell. With his thumb on the inside of her wrist, he couldn't miss the flutter of her pulse. His own echocd the rapid beat, thrumming in his veins.

"For so long, we told each other everything. All

our secrets, our hopes, our desires. We shared our highs and lows, joy and pain. The one thing we didn't share was that we were madly in love with each other."

Tears glinted in her eyes. One fell. He brushed it away with a knuckle. Damn it, did she think it was an act? Could she not see that he'd never open himself up like this were he not telling the truth?

"I promise to remind you of that every day for the rest of our lives, Sparks. To keep sharing those secrets and wishes. To hold you through the pain, the lows. To celebrate the joy, the highs. Just to be there. With you. Soaking up every last bit of life we're allotted."

Her tears were falling freely. Emma shoved a handkerchief into her hand, and she dabbed at her eyes and cheeks.

"I didn't mean to make you cry," he said quietly. "I love you."

Doubt clouded her gaze, which flicked to the camera and back to his face.

That doubt cleaved him in two. If his words didn't convince her, what would? Making this wedding legal wasn't necessary, but ensuring she knew he loved her sure was. She needed to know he wanted the elusive *forever* he'd never believed he could have. That of all the people in the world, she was the one he intended to build a life with.

Luke handed Brody the ring box.

Jack went on for a second about the symbolism of the ring having no end, just like love.

Bea went first, sliding Brody's band off her thumb. Her hands were steady. How was she calm right now?

"I give you this ring as a symbol of our love, and our unbreakable bond." She slid the ring past his knuckle.

He smiled. "Looks good there."

And he'd have to take it off soon. Nothing could be more wrong than that.

Maybe he could change this up, too. A Hail Mary in ring ceremony form. Wind teased the tops of the trees behind her, buffeting his courage.

He flicked open the box, his hands not nearly so steady as hers. The platinum band gleamed in the sunlight.

"This ring represents our love, for sure." He took her hand and positioned the band over the tip of her finger. "For however long we're given together. A day, a month, fifty years—who knows. But this ring is a reminder that the one guarantee is I'll love you. And that despite not having other guarantees, we can face the future together. It's our promises… It's my promise to put our love above my fears. To put it at the center of our lives."

Come on, Sparks. Believe me.

Her lips parted, her teeth teasing the lower one. She murmured something.

"What?" he whispered.

"Put the ring on," she said between clenched teeth. He did. Her hand flexed.

A camera winked, zoomed in on the motion.

"Stick to the script," she said, so low he doubted even Jack heard it.

Oh, no. Not anymore. He was saying goodbye to the old patterns that had defined them, the safety of being in each other's lives risk-free, being each other's safeguards and supports without committing to everything wild and wonderful. He wanted to marry this woman properly.

Private, personal.

Once they finished marrying each other today, he was going to make sure she married him for real.

Jack was talking again, but Brody only lent it half an ear.

"—kiss each other."

Right. That part.

Kissing Bea, knowing she loved him and that he'd finally figured out he could love her, too, filled him with more hope than he likely had a right to.

Her lips were soft and pliant, no hint of resistance. He clung to the possibility he still had a chance.

Wolf whistles pierced the clearing.

"Brody." Bea pulled back, expression dazed. "I think they got the picture."

Sure, but she hadn't, not yet.

It was hard not to race down the aisle, where he could finally turn off his microphone and spill all the things threatening to overflow.

They strolled past their guests. Damn it, it wasn't right that so many smiles were forced or flat.

This was not the wedding Bea deserved. She deserved to know her groom meant every word of his vows, not to be convinced of it later. To have her family share in her joy.

The second they were near the ATVs that would take the wedding party back to the lodge to prepare to greet their guests, Rashida cornered him.

"What *was that*, Brody?" she said. "Going off script?"

His cheeks tingled as the blood rushed from his head. "I'm sorry. I got carried away—"

"Sorry?" Rashida threw her arms around him. "That little show you put on is *exactly* what my viewers want. Top it with a few choice shots of you dancing at the reception and we'll be able to put this one in the bag. You fell in love on my show! That's the story I need to tell. It's not exactly what the audience is expecting, but it's real and honest and has a hell of a happy ending."

"Except it's *not* real," Bea said. "We've misled people, hurt them in the process and will have to make amends for that. Did you see my parents during the ceremony? They looked so sad, and—"

"Hey," Brody said quietly. "All we did and said up there was us being honest. I agree we have a lot of apologizing to do. But I'm not sorry for what I said at that altar. I meant every word."

Arms akimbo and with her cloak blowing in the wind, she was in fierce-warrior mode. Stick her on a flying horse, and she'd be a Valkyrie aiming a flaming spear at his head. "Your vows were true? But you told me… You said you loved me."

"Because I do." He'd fall to his knees and swear it if he had to.

She let out a disbelieving laugh. "You're so scared of being in love, you're *sweating*. Outside. In November." She motioned to his forehead, which, yeah, was a bit damp.

"I'm not scared to love you," he explained. "I'm scared of losing you. Except…if I don't love you, I'll guaranteed lose you. Or at least lose the true possibility of a future together. My life doesn't work without you, Beatrix."

So many emotions bent her expression that her face went almost blank, like the combination canceled itself out.

She shook her head. "You know, you've always told me, or at least implied, that I'm enough. But that can't be true. Not when it comes to the kind of commitment involved in a marriage. And I'm okay with that. We'll get through the reception and go back to Seattle. Pretend none of this happened."

"There's no pretending we didn't fall in love with each other! Bea, I'm not going to say that our feelings changing means the end of our friendship. We've been friends too long not to find a way to keep it. Which—it *is* enough. Just like you are. But since when are you satisfied with *settling*?"

She blinked, eyes glinting a luminous green. "You're saying…"

"I'm in love with you, Bea. And I *want* to be married to you."

"Convenient." She looked down at her ring. "We are married. Or would be, if we filed the paperwork. Which we aren't going to do."

And she looked so, so sad about that.

He lifted her hand and kissed her finger, the metal of her wedding band cold against his lips. His grandmother's diamonds were hard and smooth, five little reminders that they had so much to emulate. "It wasn't conventional. Which is kinda perfect—an unusual start to an unusual life."

"No," Bea said, pointing at her cousin, who was approaching from down the trail. "Do not fill out your part of the marriage license."

Jack tripped over a root, barely righting himself in time to avoid eating dirt. He winced, rubbing his shoulder. "What the hell are you talking about?"

"Tell the story how you want to, Rashida. We owe you that much." She sent Brody a help-me-out look. "But the ceremony today. It can't count."

"It has to," Rashida reminded them, looking oddly uncomfortable to be witnessing their private moment. She also looked supremely apologetic. "Remember what I said? The contract requires a legal marriage."

Bea clutched his hand, staring into his eyes. "I'm going to have to break it, then."

Chapter Seventeen

The way Brody's face fell at Bea's pronouncement, she could almost believe he loved her.

"You don't mean that," he said. "You can't owe the money. Not after everything we did this week."

"It's just money, Brody. And a business is just a business. It doesn't define who I am. And if I fail at this business, then at least my family can love me for owning up to my mistakes rather than being a liar."

"Marrying me was a mistake?" Devastation ravaged his face.

"This wedding was," she whispered.

"But...but you wanted me to be open to love. And I did that, I fell for you, I proclaimed it in front of the most important people in our lives, and..."

"And how am I supposed to believe it's true, when it's wrapped up with all our dishonesty?"

There was the Brody she thought she knew—reliable, a support, but walled off from feelings and romantic commitment—and the Brody before her now, spilling out words with an utter lack of abandon. The two collided in her brain like a derailing train, sending up sparks and smoke and a screeching cacophony.

She wanted to run into the forest, far from their confused guests and family, their annoyed producer, her pleading groom. Far enough into the wilderness to avoid processing all those gorgeous, terrible words he'd said during his impromptu vows.

The forest they explored as kids was silent, not giving any wisdom. "I don't... I just..."

"Did I misunderstand you when you said you'd fallen in love with me? I mean, I guess that could be the truth but also you still don't want to be with me?" His words were a rush of panic. "Or maybe it's too fast. Is it too fast? We can take marriage off the table. For as long as you want it to be. I just... I want to love you, Bea. Please, trust me to do that."

"How can I? You can't just change from anti-marriage to desperate to spend your life with me with a snap of your fingers."

"Who said it was sudden? I planned a wedding with my best friend. Kissed her. Made love with her. Said vows—"

"Fake vows."

"No. As real as they get. And I was finally able to see that what I'm feeling is love. Those words—they held a magnifying glass up to my fears. And today, hearing you be courageous and seeing you as a bride and standing at that altar with you? Nothing's ever felt so right. Wasn't it the same for you?"

"For a moment? Yes." How could it not be? The fantasy of being with him, of her best friend becoming her everything.

His throat bobbed. "Coming from me, I get it doesn't make sense. Wanting more all of a sudden. Wanting to feel every feeling, share every risk. No longer limiting our feelings or living in a safe box. You love squeezing out every last drop from life. Let's do that together, by loving each other with no limits."

Her hands shook, and she reached for his. The steadiness with which he met her, warm palms, strong grip, enough to carry them through a lifetime. She'd been the one telling Brody that there were no guarantees but that was okay, that life was still worth living. And here *she* was, pushing back, not believing in the beauty of what he was telling her. Why? That nagging fear she wasn't enough?

She'd been enough for him to open up in front of all their loved ones. And if he was going to push past his fear, then she'd do the same. "You really mean it."

"I do," he said.

I do. A chill washed over her. "Like I said, this can't be our wedding. I love you. I want to build a life with you. And we deserve better than this. Than going through our wedding ceremony with doubt in our hearts. Having our families confused and frowning in the audience. Having fricking cameras recording our promises."

He cupped her cheeks. "You don't want this wedding to count, Beatrix? Fine, we won't file the paperwork, and we'll figure out a way to pay the contract money. But please. *Please* believe me that I love you."

Rising on her toes, she kissed him. Pressed into his hard frame and clung to his shoulders. And unlike the kiss they'd shared at the altar, she knew it was real.

Someone coughed. Bea startled.

Jack, standing a few yards away with Rashida, the two of them mostly turned to at least pretend to give Bea and Brody some privacy.

"Yes?" Bea asked as Brody pulled her back to his front, wrapping her cloak around her and ensconcing her in a world of warmth.

"You have thirty days to register your marriage, you know," Jack said.

"Good try." She burrowed deeper against Brody. "Doesn't matter how many days pass, this is never going to feel like 'our' wedding."

"So, marry me again, sweetheart." Brody's lips dipped to her ear, brushing the sensitive flesh. "On Christmas Eve. That's what, twenty-six days away? Then we can file the license."

She froze. "Marry you again?"

"If…if that's what you want."

Waking up on Christmas Day actually married to Brody, feeling like the ring on her finger belonged? It seemed too good to be true.

And it was very much in her grasp to make it her reality. "That is what I want, Brody. I want to make plans for the new year as a committed couple. As your wife."

"Then let's go hold our reception. And in a few weeks, we'll come back here and get married."

She laughed. "That's the wrong order."

"So was getting engaged and then falling in love, but I don't mind doing things backward, as long as it means I get to spend my life with you."

Epilogue

December 23

"Oh! I know you two," the flight attendant said, passing over the glasses of champagne. "The first-class virgin! But also, I watched your wedding last night. It was *beautiful*. And the flowers…to die for. I can't believe you did the arrangements for your own wedding."

Brody kissed one of Bea's blushing cheeks and nodded at the familiar woman as he took the flutes. They were at thirty-two thousand feet, and Bea was insistent that this time, she wasn't going to miss out on the complimentary bubbles in the primo seating.

"Yeah," he said. "You were our flight attendant

the last time we flew to Bozeman." He glanced at her name tag. "Hilary. It was definitely you."

The flight attendant leaned in, like she was eager for a secret. "Is it true? The fake-it-until-you-make-it routine?"

"Yes. True. Not a line to gain ratings." Bea sipped her champagne. She looked a little tired, probably because she'd been so damn busy this week at work. Since the episode went live, her phone had rung off the hook. Some of the calls were lookie-loos wondering about the fake-engagement-turned-real tale Rashida had spun, but most were new clients. She was booking well into the following summer.

He was so proud of her, of getting to be with her.

Every day she came home to their town house, smelling of fresh greenery and the fabric softener that was now theirs instead of his, and he learned a little more about being her partner as well as her friend. It was like putting on glasses for the first time. He was quickly getting used to crisp edges, clarity, tiny details previously missed.

Sliding his fingers through hers, he murmured, "I love you."

"I love you, too."

"And to think, I almost missed the chance to hear you say that."

She turned and nuzzled her head in the crook of his neck and shoulder. "And waking up with me in your arms, or getting to trade silly grins in first class. Really, you're lucky we found our holiday miracle."

Chuckling, he threaded his fingers through her hair and kissed her crown. "No, I'm lucky you were brave as hell, and were patient enough to wait for me to catch up."

"You always were good at coming from behind in the final five hundred," she teased.

He laughed.

"Going home for Christmas?" Hilary asked on her way up the aisle.

Bea shook her head and looked at Brody, eyes glinting. "We're getting married."

Hilary's blond brows disappeared under her bangs. "But..."

"We ran into a snag with the paperwork the first time around," Brody explained, sticking with the story they'd decided to use with people who didn't need to know the whole truth. "But the bonus is, I get to tell the world how much I love this woman twice."

"Will it be on *DIY I Do*, too?" Hilary's smile emitted enough fascination to light the entire first-class cabin.

"No," Bea said, tone secretive and satisfied. "This one's going to be just for us."

Well, for them and their forty closest family members and friends, who filled the great hall of the wilderness lodge the following day. Christmas Eve.

They'd blended the lodge's holiday motif with Bea's need for some nontraditional color in a vintage decoration theme—rich, saturated pinks, yellows and blues among the greens and reds. She was already making noise about using some of the decorations in their town house the following year. Just the thought of making their own Christmas traditions widened the grin on his face.

His lovesick expression earned him an elbow from his cousin, who sat next to him at the head table.

"You proved me wrong, and I couldn't be happier about it," Luke said.

"Proved me wrong, too," he said, glancing to his right and winking at his colorfully dressed bride. She'd surprised everyone by deciding not to carry flowers for the ceremony. Instead, she'd chosen a flowy gown splashed with a kaleidoscope of blooms.

Emma, who was standing at the microphone, wore a short, loudly fuchsia number to coordinate. Nora's was a vibrant violet.

But Bea's laugh was the brightest thing in the great hall. The wedding party could be wearing T-shirts and shorts and standing in a bare room—as long as she laughed like that, he'd have all his hopes for the day fulfilled.

"I would only move the traditional Twelve Days twelfth-day open house for a handful of people, you know," Emma teased them, she and Nora holding the guests captive with their joint speech. "But being able to make sure your day was perfect makes this the best Christmas in a long time. We all deserve second chances sometimes." She sent Luke a long, warm look that he returned.

Bea leaned to Brody's ear. "This second chance is perfect."

"It could never be anything less," he whispered back.

"Who knew Bea would like getting married so much she'd end up doing it twice?" Emma's eyes sparkled. Where the sisters' speech at the *DIY I Do* reception had been full of generic platitudes, this one was far more irreverent. The two were all about giving Bea and Brody the gears, now that they weren't being filmed.

"She can have my share," Nora joked. "Everyone knows I won't be getting near an altar anytime soon."

Brody had no doubt that was true—his perfectionist sister-in-law's unreasonably high demands were legendary—but there was a flicker of sadness in Nora's blue eyes that made him wonder what her real feelings were on the matter.

"I highly recommend marrying your best friend," Bea called out, squeezing his hand.

"Or your longtime rival." Emma winked at Luke.

"Or your childhood crush," his brother-in-law, Graydon, added from one of the tables where he sat with his wife, Alejandra. They each held one of their twins on their lap, the babies looking adorable in matching satin dresses.

Brody returned Bea's hand squeeze and nodded in the direction of the twins. "One day? After we travel to some exciting places and make a home?"

"Sounds like the biggest adventure of all."

He took a mental picture of her smile, one he'd pull out on the inevitable challenging days. But no matter what, they'd get through them together. "Can't wait to explore with you, Beatrix. Find all the newness life has to offer."

"The old is pretty good, too," she said.

"Loving my best friend seems like the foundation my life needs," he said, every word as much of a vow as the ones they'd said an hour ago in front of the tall river-rock fireplace anchoring the great hall. "I'll keep my feet on the ground. You can reach for the stars."

* * * * *

Sutter Creek, Montana miniseries:

From Exes to Expecting
A Father for Her Child
Holiday by Candlelight
Their Nine-Month Surprise
In Service of Love
Snowbound with the Sheriff
Twelve Dates of Christmas
What to Expect When She's Expecting

Available now from Harlequin Special Edition!

#2953 A FORTUNE'S WINDFALL
The Fortunes of Texas: Hitting the Jackpot • by Michelle Major
When Linc Maloney inherits a fortune, he throws caution to the wind and vows to live life like there's no tomorrow. His friend and former coworker Remi Reynolds thinks that Linc is out of control and tries to remind him that money can't buy happiness. She can't admit to herself that she's been feeling more than *like* for Linc for a long time but doesn't dare risk her heart on a man with a big-as-Texas fear of commitment...

#2954 HER BEST FRIEND'S BABY
Sierra's Web • by Tara Taylor Quinn
Child psychiatrist Megan Latimer would trust family attorney Daniel Tremaine with her life—but never her heart. Danny's far too attractive for any woman's good...until one night changes everything. As if crossing the line weren't cataclysmic enough, Megan and Danny just went from besties and colleagues to parents-to-be. As they work together to resolve a complex custody case, can they save a family and find their own happily-ever-after?

#2955 FALLING FOR HIS FAKE GIRLFRIEND
Sutton's Place • by Shannon Stacey
Over-the-top Molly Cyrs hardly seems a match for bookish Callan Avery. But when Molly suggests they pose as a couple to assuage Stonefield's anxiety about its new male librarian, his pretend paramour is all Callan can think about. Callan's looking for a family, though, and kids aren't in Molly's story. Unless he can convince Molly that she's not "too much"...and that to him, she's just enough!

#2956 THE BOOKSTORE'S SECRET
Home to Oak Hollow • by Makenna Lee
Aspiring pastry chef Nicole Evans is just waiting to hear about her dream job, and in the meantime, she goes to work in the café at the local bookstore. But that's before the recently widowed Nicole meets her temporary boss: her first crush, Liam Mendez! Will his simmering attraction to Nicole be just one more thing to hide...or the stuff of his bookstore's romance novels?

#2957 THEIR SWEET COASTAL REUNION
Sisters of Christmas Bay • by Kaylie Newell
When Kyla Beckett returns to Christmas Bay to help her foster mom, the last person she wants to run into is Ben Martinez. The small-town police chief just wants a second chance—to explain. But when Ben's little girl bonds with his longtime frenemy, he wonders if it might be the start of a friendship. Can the wounded single dad convince Kyla he's always wanted the best for her...then, now and forever?

#2958 A HERO AND HIS DOG
Small-Town Sweethearts • by Carrie Nichols
Former Special Forces soldier Mitch Sawicki's mission is simple: find the dog who survived the explosion that ended Mitch's military career. Vermont farmer Aurora Walsh thinks Mitch is the extra pair of hands she desperately needs. Her young daughter sees Mitch as a welcome addition to their family, whose newest member is the three-legged Sarge. Can another wounded warrior find a home with a pint-size princess and her irresistible mother?

YOU CAN FIND MORE INFORMATION ON UPCOMING HARLEQUIN TITLES, FREE EXCERPTS AND MORE AT HARLEQUIN.COM.

HSECNM1122

Get 4 FREE REWARDS!

We'll send you 2 FREE Books plus 2 FREE Mystery Gifts.

FREE
Value Over
$20

Both the **Harlequin® Special Edition** and **Harlequin® Heartwarming™** series feature compelling novels filled with stories of love and strength where the bonds of friendship, family and community unite.

YES! Please send me 2 FREE novels from the Harlequin Special Edition or Harlequin Heartwarming series and my 2 FREE gifts (gifts are worth about $10 retail). After receiving them, if I don't wish to receive any more books, I can return the shipping statement marked "cancel." If I don't cancel, I will receive 6 brand-new Harlequin Special Edition books every month and be billed just $5.49 each in the U.S. or $6.24 each in Canada, a savings of at least 12% off the cover price, or 4 brand-new Harlequin Heartwarming Larger-Print books every month and be billed just $6.24 each in the U.S. or $6.74 each in Canada, a savings of at least 19% off the cover price. It's quite a bargain! Shipping and handling is just 50¢ per book in the U.S. and $1.25 per book in Canada.* I understand that accepting the 2 free books and gifts places me under no obligation to buy anything. I can always return a shipment and cancel at any time by calling the number below. The free books and gifts are mine to keep no matter what I decide.

Choose one: ☐ **Harlequin Special Edition**   ☐ **Harlequin Heartwarming**
                        (235/335 HDN GRJV)   **Larger-Print**
                                                    (161/361 HDN GRJV)

Name (please print)

Address   Apt. #

City   State/Province   Zip/Postal Code

Email: Please check this box ☐ if you would like to receive newsletters and promotional emails from Harlequin Enterprises ULC and its affiliates. You can unsubscribe anytime.

Mail to the **Harlequin Reader Service:**
IN U.S.A.: P.O. Box 1341, Buffalo, NY 14240-8531
IN CANADA: P.O. Box 603, Fort Erie, Ontario L2A 5X3

Want to try 2 free books from another series! Call **1-800-873-8635** or visit www.ReaderService.com.

*Terms and prices subject to change without notice. Prices do not include sales taxes, which will be charged (if applicable) based on your state or country of residence. Canadian residents will be charged applicable taxes. Offer not valid in Quebec. This offer is limited to one order per household. Books received may not be as shown. Not valid for current subscribers to the Harlequin Special Edition or Harlequin Heartwarming series. All orders subject to approval. Credit or debit balances in a customer's account(s) may be offset by any other outstanding balance owed by or to the customer. Please allow 4 to 6 weeks for delivery. Offer available while quantities last.

Your Privacy—Your information is being collected by Harlequin Enterprises ULC, operating as Harlequin Reader Service. For a complete summary of the information we collect, how we use this information and to whom it is disclosed, please visit our privacy notice located at corporate.harlequin.com/privacy-notice. From time to time we may also exchange your personal information with reputable third parties. If you wish to opt out of this sharing of your personal information, please visit readerservice.com/consumerschoice or call 1-800-873-8635. **Notice to California Residents**—Under California law, you have specific rights to control and access your data. For more information on these rights and how to exercise them, visit corporate.harlequin.com/california-privacy.

HSEHW22R3

HARLEQUIN
PLUS

Announcing a **BRAND-NEW** multimedia subscription service for romance fans like you!

Read, Watch and Play.

Experience the easiest way to get the romance content you crave.

Start your **FREE 7 DAY TRIAL** at
<u>www.harlequinplus.com/freetrial</u>.

HARPLUS0822